SCARY STORIES

FOR SLEEP-OVERS #9

By Allen B. Ury

ROXBURY PARK

LOWELL HOUSE JUVENILE

LOS ANGELES

NTC/Contemporary Publishing Group

For Robert
–A.B.U.

Published by Lowell House
A division of NTC/Contemporary Publishing Group, Inc.
4255 West Touhy Ave, Lincolnwood (Chicago), Illinois 06046-1975 U.S.A.
© 1998 by NTC/Contemporary Publishing Group, Inc.

ISBN: 1-56565-895-7
Library of Congress Catalog Card Number: 98-066241

Requests for such permissions should be addressed to:

Lowell House
2020 Avenue of the Stars, Suite 300
Los Angeles, CA 90067

Lowell House books can be purchased at special discounts when ordered in bulk for premiums and special sales.
Contact Customer Service at NTC/Contemporary Publishing Group, Inc.
4255 W. Touhy Avenue Lincolnwood, IL 60646-1975
1-800-323-4900

Managing Director & Publisher: Jack Artenstein
Editor in Chief, Roxbury Park Books: Michael Artenstein
Director of Publishing Services: Rena Copperman
Managing Editor: Lindsey Hay
Cover illustration: Dwight Been

Printed and bound in the United States of America
10 9 8 7 6 5 4 3

Contents

The Boy Inside

"Hey, dogface! Why don't you go chase a rabbit?" one of Jerry Elfman's classmates taunted.

"Wow, the last time I saw ears *that* big, they were on an elephant!" another one of the eleven-year-olds snickered.

"And look at that nose!" chided a third fifth-grader. "It looks like he's got a cucumber between his eyes!"

"You just gonna sit there and take that, Jerry?" asked Ben Taggart, Jerry's best—and only—friend at Piedmont Junior High. "You oughta say something back!"

Jerry bowed his head, keeping his eyes fixed on the chicken salad sandwich on the lunch table in front of him.

"They'll just beat me up," Jerry whispered, his voice nearly choking from emotion. "And then they'll really make fun of me." He shrugged his shoulder in the direction of the three bullies seated at the next lunch table but was careful to avoid eye contact with any of them.

"Boy, when they were handing out ugly, you must've gone back for seconds!" said Michael Malik, Jerry's chief tormentor. Although Michael was a month younger than Jerry, the bully had a good two inches and twenty pounds on him, and Jerry knew better than to challenge him physically.

"Oh, why don't you just back off!" Ben finally shot back.

"Ben, don't" Jerry grunted through clenched teeth. He grabbed his friend's wrist in a vain attempt to keep the situation from getting worse.

"What did you say, Taggart?" Michael demanded, rising to his feet. His two friends stood up as well, their hands balling into fists. They were obviously itching for a fight, and Ben had just given them an excuse.

"I told you to back off!" Ben replied defiantly. "That's really stupid to make fun of somebody's looks. You think Jerry can help it if he's ugly? Do you think he *likes* going around with a face like a basset hound? Do you?"

"Some friend you got there, Elfman," another of the bullies snickered. "He says you got a face like a basset hound!"

"Actually, I'd say more like a dachshund," the third bully said, studying Jerry's face the way a scientist might study a curious freak of nature. "Or maybe a beagle."

"Someone oughta lock you up in a kennel and throw away the key," Michael said. "Ah-wooooo!" He howled like a coyote baying at the moon. His two friends joined in, and then some kids at the next table took up the call. Within seconds the entire cafeteria was echoing with barks, snarls, and yips. It sounded like a pack of wolves had suddenly gone stark raving mad. And in the center of it was Jerry Elfman. He sat silently with his head bowed in shame, wishing he could crawl into a hole and die.

....

"You can't let those boys get to you," Jerry's mother said later that day. "They only have as much power as you give them, you know."

"They said I was ugly, that I looked like a dog," Jerry grumbled. He caught a glimpse of his reflection in the entry-hall mirror. Even *he* had to admit that he did bear an uncanny resemblance to a canine. His face was unusually long and drawn for an eleven-year-old, with a narrow, pronounced nose and large ears that, if seen from the proper angle, seemed to almost come to a point. His eyelids also tended to sag, which gave him the look of a tired bloodhound. "The thing is, they're right. I *do* look like a dog. I'm ugly."

"Kids can be so cruel," his mother said, shaking her head in dismay. "What you don't realize is that beauty is only skin-deep. If they only bothered to look harder, they'd see the handsome boy that's inside you."

"Well, I wish he'd come out already." Jerry groaned impatiently. "'Cause this ugly one here on the outside is getting tired of being laughed at all the time. And I'm getting tired of looking at him."

"Oh, he'll come out, all right," his mother promised. "Just like the story of the ugly duckling. You wait and see.

Someday you'll wake up and discover that you've been turned into a beautiful swan."

Great, Jerry thought. *Just what I need. Next I'm going to look like a bird!*

. . . .

Jerry was sitting at the dining room table doing his homework when the first sensation hit. It felt like an odd tingling in his fingertips, as if thousands of ants were crawling over them. Jerry set down his pencil and shook out his hands. *Writer's cramp*, he thought, then returned to his studies. But the tingling continued, now spreading up his fingers to his palms and wrists. Now he rubbed his hands together, as if trying to restore circulation. He was reminded of the times he'd sat in front of his living room TV, his head propped up on one hand, only to have that hand fall asleep and become uncomfortably numb and awkward. When circulation returned to the hand, the painful tingling was not unlike the sensation he was experiencing now. The only difference was, he hadn't been putting any pressure on his hand—and this time *both* hands were affected.

"Ouch!" Jerry cried aloud as the painful tingling now spread up his arms to his shoulders. The "ants" he initially imagined were now swarming all over him, pricking his body with their tiny stingers. *What's going on?* he thought fearfully. *What's happening to me?*

Abandoning his work, Jerry jumped to his feet and ran into the nearby kitchen where his mother was busy preparing chicken for their dinner. Already he could feel the tingling moving into his chest and neck. Meanwhile, his fingers, which had been the first to feel the sensation, had begun to feel cold and numb, like they'd just spent the past hour packed in ice.

"Mom, something's happening to me!" he managed to choke out.

"What?" his mother replied, caught by surprise. She turned away from the cooking island and immediately saw the terror on her son's face. "Honey, what's wrong?"

"I don't know!" Jerry said, his eyes filling with tears. "I can't feel my hands! Or my arms!" He tried to lift his hands toward her but suddenly realized to his horror that he couldn't even feel them on his body!

"When did this start?" his mother asked, hurrying toward him.

"Just a minute ago," Jerry gasped. He was having difficulty breathing now. The strange tingling had now gripped his chest and was moving rapidly to his stomach. He realized that it would soon reach his legs, at which point he didn't know if he'd even be able to stand. "Mom, you'd better call nine-one-one. Something horrible is happening to me!"

"Now, now, calm down," his mother said soothingly. "I'm sure you're going to be fine. How 'bout you lie down on the couch and see how you feel in a few minutes. It's probably just the beginning of the flu."

Jerry wanted to believe his mother. He hoped that this *was* just the onset of the flu. But this wasn't like any flu he'd ever experienced, and he'd been knocked out with the worst of them.

"Okay," he said with a sigh. He turned toward the

living room, but as he did, his head began to swim. The house appeared to whirl crazily around him, and he immediately lost his balance.

"Jerry!" he heard his mother scream. The next moment he was staring up at her from the kitchen floor. If he'd hurt himself when he fell, he never felt it.

············

The harsh fluorescent lights shone directly into Jerry's face. He wanted desperately to turn away, to shield his eyes from their painful brightness, but he was unable to lift his arms or even move his head. In fact, he couldn't even feel his body around him. It was as if he were floating in a warm pool, his face turned toward the sun, his entire being blending perfectly with his surroundings. But this was no comforting pool he was lying in. It was a hospital bed. And he was surrounded by a dozen cold machines, each one responsible for keeping some part of his failing body alive.

After what seemed like an eternity in this terrifying state, he became aware of movement around him. He tried to turn his head, but no matter how hard he tried, the overhead fluorescent light refused to move from its position directly above him. Finally his mother, his father, and a gray-bearded doctor he remembered seeing soon after his arrival here at the hospital appeared overhead. As they peered down at him, Jerry felt like he was at the bottom of a well looking up at distant faces far beyond his reach.

"Jerry, honey, can you hear us?" his mother asked.

Yes, I can hear you, Jerry thought. *I can hear you just fine.*

The only problem was, he couldn't find enough strength to move his lips to respond.

"He can hear you, Mrs. Elfman," the doctor assured her. "The EKG readings show that his brain is still functioning perfectly."

"Jerry, the doctors think they know what's wrong with you," his father said, struggling to form a smile. "Dr. Kreisant, why don't you tell him."

"Well, Jerry, it's like this," the doctor began, his voice stern and serious. "You have a tumor growing on your spinal column. It's blocking the normal flow of electrical impulses through your nervous system. We did a biopsy— that is, we took a sample of the tumor—and it doesn't appear to be cancerous. That's the good news."

If Jerry could have breathed a sigh of relief, that's exactly what he would have done at this point.

"The bad news is, although all the tumor's cells are healthy, it's continuing to grow at an extremely rapid rate," Dr. Kreisant continued. "I don't know what else to tell you. It's like nothing we've seen before. We don't know how long the tumor will continue to grow, or how long your body will be able to coexist with it. All we know is that we can't operate without leaving you permanently paralyzed. We have some experimental drugs we'd like to try, but to be honest with you, all we can really do is wait, pray, and see what happens."

If Jerry could have felt the skin on his face, he'd have sensed that a tear was running down his right cheek.

....

A full week had passed since Jerry had been admitted to the hospital. During that time he'd been poked, prodded, and examined with instruments he couldn't even begin to understand. But despite the best that modern medical science could do, the doctors had been unable to stop the tumor's relentless growth. It appeared that the boy was doomed.

"I'm sorry," Jerry heard Dr. Kreisant tell his parents after the last barrage of experimental drugs had failed to have any effect. "We've done our best. The tumor is now occupying over eighty percent of your son's abdominal cavity. It's putting tremendous pressure on his internal organs. He could go at any time."

He could hear his mother sobbing somewhere behind him. He found it strange that, despite the horror that was infesting his body, he felt absolutely no pain or discomfort. Perhaps the paralysis was a blessing in disguise.

"There is one odd thing, though . . ." Dr. Kreisant continued.

"What?" Jerry's father asked, grasping at any glimmer of hope.

"The tumor itself is extraordinary," the physician noted. "It's not the random collection of cells we normally find in these cases. It seems to have a definite structure."

"Structure? What do you mean, structure?" Jerry's father asked impatiently.

"Well, it appears to be organized in a definite pattern," Dr. Kreisant began. But before he could continue, he was cut short by Mrs. Elfman's terrified scream.

If Jerry could have seen what was happening around him, he'd have seen his mother pointing directly at him, her face filled with terror. He'd have seen his father and Dr. Kreisant turn as well, their jaws drop, and their eyes open as wide as saucers. And if he could have seen himself, he'd have understood the reason for their reactions. Something was happening to his body. Something awful. His skin, which had been steadily dehydrating since he'd come to the hospital, had begun to crack and peel. Deep fissures were erupting all over his body. Then, incredibly, his skin began to peel back from his face, torso, and limbs like the skin being ripped off an orange. Something was forcing itself out from within his body—something dark, wet, and covered with reddish ooze.

"We need a crash team in here, stat!" Dr. Kreisant shouted.

"What's happening to him?" Jerry's father demanded.

"What is that—*thing*?" his mother gasped.

Suddenly, for the first time in a week, Jerry became aware of his arms and legs. His flexed his fingers, tensed his arm muscles, and wiggled his toes.

"Mom? Dad?" he gasped, his voice weak and raspy from inactivity.

His muscles painfully stiff, he sat up in bed and became aware that he was covered from head to toe with a reddish jellylike substance. The stuff smelled foul, and he tried to brush it off his bare arms. It was then that he saw something lying on the floor at the foot of his bed, something he at first couldn't quite make out. It appeared to be some kind of flesh-covered fabric, one that had been ripped and torn by a wild animal. He nearly fainted when he realized he was looking down at his own skin.

"Jerry, are you okay?" his mother asked desperately.

"I'm fine . . ." he whispered, not quite certain *how* he felt.

"How are you feeling?" his mother asked.

"Is that really you, son?" his father asked curiously.

"What do you mean?" he replied.

Her hand shaking, his mother held a makeup mirror in front of Jerry's face. He brushed the jellylike goo off his cheeks and forehead, and tried to wipe the awful stuff out of his hair. Although he was still coated with the slime, he quickly understood the reason for his parents' confusion. His once-prominent nose had shrunk by half. His cheekbones had risen, and his once slack jaw had become sharp and firm. Not only that, but the scrawny chest and flabby stomach he'd always known had suddenly turned hard and muscular. No, not *turned*. They had been *replaced*! He'd suddenly become *handsome*!

"The tumor . . ." he gasped in sudden comprehension. "The thing that was growing inside me. It wasn't a tumor at all. It was a whole new body!"

"It must be a kind of metamorphosis," Jerry's dad speculated. "Like a caterpillar turning into a butterfly."

"Or an ugly duckling becoming a beautiful swan," Jerry's mother said, smiling.

Jerry smiled, too. His mom had always talked about the handsome boy inside him. Now, at long last, it had revealed itself.

A four-person medical team arrived with various emergency gear. They looked to Dr. Kreisant for instructions.

"The emergency's over," the doctor said. "Let's give this boy a shower and clean him up. Then I want to start a new series of tests. We're going to figure out just what the heck happened here!"

Suddenly brimming with energy, Jerry offered his arms to the medical personnel as they helped him off the bed.

"Boy," he said with a grin. "Wait 'til the kids at school see me now!" His mind began to spin with all the possibilities. *I'll show them! Now I'll be the best-looking! Now I'll be the one who—*

He took a step toward the door and suddenly felt his legs collapse beneath him.

"Are you okay?" his mother asked with alarm.

"I—I don't know," Jerry stammered. "I can't feel my legs again!"

The awful tingling sensation had returned. It washed over his body like a powerful wave, causing him to go numb all over.

"Get him down to MRI, stat," Dr. Kreisant ordered. "I want a fully body scan. Hurry!"

But Jerry didn't need to see the results of any tests to know what was happening to him. He could sense that there was another tumor already inside him. It was on his spine, choking off his nerves and blood vessels.

And it was growing.

The Girl in the Attic

I knew there was something strange about the vacation cabin the minute I saw it. It certainly wasn't the building's classic log cabin design, its location on the northern shore of Wisconsin's Lake Waupaca, or its freshly painted exterior. In fact, from an objective point of view, the house was as beautiful as anything out of a picture postcard. No, it was the *feeling* I got when we pulled up the gravel path and first saw the rustic, two-story home that convinced me that something here was very, very wrong. I felt cold. Clammy. It was the same unsettled feeling you might get when looking down into a dank, unlit basement or driving past a cemetery at night. It creeped me out.

My fear must have been obvious on my face, because my

younger sister, Sara, spoke up even before our dad stopped the van.

"What's wrong, Lisa?" she asked. "You see something, don't you?"

This wasn't an unusual question for Sara to ask me. All my life, I'd been famous for my "heightened senses." I'd always been able to see things that were too far away for most other people to see without binoculars, or too small for "normal" folks to spot without a magnifying glass. Supposedly my hearing was as good as most dogs', and my elevated senses of taste and smell had made me a *very* fussy eater, ever since I was a baby. Because I noticed things that other people couldn't see or just tended to ignore, Sara had come to depend on me to act as an "early warning system" whenever we went somewhere new.

"It's the cabin," I said softly, keeping my eyes fixed on the attractive, well-maintained structure.

"What about it?" Dad asked, turning around to look at me. "You see termites or something?" My father was also well aware of my special "powers" but usually made them the butt of good-natured jokes. The last thing he wanted me to feel like was some kind of a freak.

"No, it looks fine," I replied. "I just get the feeling—" I stopped. I didn't know how to put my misgivings into words the others would understand. Finally I forced a smile. "I get the feeling we're going to have a great time here."

"I sure hope so," Mom said with a sigh of relief. "We're sure paying enough for this place!"

···········

The lakeside cabin, which my parents had rented through a travel agent, was actually pretty small on the inside. The downstairs consisted of basically one big living room that had a kitchenette in one corner. A sofa and several chairs were grouped around a stone fireplace, and in another corner stood a small TV equipped with a VCR.

A staircase took you up to the second-floor landing. There were two bedrooms up there. Mom and Dad were to sleep in one, and Sara and I would share the other.

Although the cabin wasn't fancy, it was clean and definitely cozy. Most people would see it as a great place to spend a relaxing week away from the noise and pressure of the city. But I couldn't shake the uneasy feeling that there was something, well, *wrong* about this house. Something that carried the stench of death.

Since I had nothing to back up my suspicions, I kept up a happy front as we all unpacked and got ready for dinner. But as I was helping Mom prepare some ground beef we'd brought from home, I heard something that immediately shattered any hopes I may have had that this was going to be a normal family outing.

"Help!" I heard someone scream. "Help me! Please! Don't let me die!"

I immediately turned away from the kitchen counter. The voice was a girl's. She was scared out of her mind. And she sounded very, very close.

"Help me!" I heard her scream again. "I'm up here!"

I immediately turned to my mom.

"Did you hear that?" I asked urgently.

"Hear what?" Mom replied, her concentration on the mass of ground beef she was mixing with eggs and seasonings.

"There's a girl shouting for help!" I said. "We've got to do something!"

I ran to the front window but could see nothing but our car in the driveway, the thick woods, and the shimmering lake beyond.

"What's going on?" my dad asked, coming down the stairs, with Sara close behind.

"Lisa thinks she heard a girl calling for help," Mom told him, a nervous twinge to her voice.

"Well, let's go take a look," said Dad as he headed for the front door.

Dad, Sara, and I assembled outside the house. As this was early July, the sun was still high in the sky and the air was pleasantly warm. I strained to listen, but all I could hear was the chirping of birds and the rustling of leaves in the gentle wind.

"Well?" Dad asked. "You still hear it?"

"Not anymore," I confessed.

"Maybe the girl was calling from another cabin," Sara suggested.

"I don't think there's another cabin around here for at least a quarter mile," Dad said. "Lisa's hearing may be good, but it's not *that* good."

"Besides, it didn't sound far away," I said. "It sounded close. Almost as if it were coming from inside the house."

"Let's look around," said Sara. "Maybe she's around here somewhere."

"Don't go far," Dad warned. "We don't want you getting lost in the forest on your first day."

"We won't," I said and began to lead Sara around to the back of the cabin. My sister and I explored the thick woods around the house for almost a half hour until Mom called us in to set the table for dinner. We saw no sign of people anywhere, let alone a girl in trouble.

It was so strange. I *knew* I'd heard the cries for help. They weren't just my imagination. But what could I do about it? Finally I decided to just let it go. If a girl had gotten into trouble, maybe we'd read about it in the local paper—if there even *was* such a thing out here so many miles from civilization.

···········

Things passed pretty uneventfully for the next few days. Sara and I went fishing with Dad on the lake. I actually caught a four-pound bass, while Sara's catches consisted mostly of little sunfish, which Dad made her throw back. We all went hiking in the woods, and Mom spent a lot of time painting landscapes.

And then, on our fifth day at the cabin, I was running up to my room to get a sweatshirt when I again heard the girl's voice.

"Help!" she shouted. "Help me, please! I'm up here! In the attic! You've got to let me out! Someone! Please! Don't let me die!"

Terrified, I immediately bolted back downstairs where the rest of my family was waiting.

"She's upstairs! She's in the attic!" I shouted in alarm.

"Who's upstairs?" Mom asked.

"The girl I heard the other day!" I said, realizing how strange I sounded even as I said it. "She's stuck in the attic! We've got to let her out!"

"How could a girl get in our attic?" Sara asked skeptically. "Wouldn't we have seen her?"

"I don't know, but I just heard her," I insisted. "Dad, please, we have to go up there!"

"All right, I'll check the attic," Dad said with a sigh. "But if there's a girl trapped up there, I'll be very, very surprised."

Moving as one, we all went up the stairs to the second floor. Gathering on the landing, we looked up at the hinged ceiling panel that led to the attic above.

"Hello?" Dad called, his hands cupped around his mouth. "Is anybody up there?"

The response was nothing but eerie silence.

"There's nobody up there," Sara stated. "This time, Lisa, I think you've been hearing things."

"I know what I heard," I insisted. "If nobody else will go up there, *I* will."

"I'll check," Dad volunteered. "Everybody, stand back."

He opened the nearby linen closet and pulled out a four-foot-long wooden pole with a hook on the end. He looped the hook through the handle in the ceiling panel and pulled. A spring-loaded latch released, the panel swung down like a hinged door, and a ladder dropped out.

"Hello!" I called up through the dark, narrow opening. There was still no response.

"Here, dear," said Mom, handing Dad a flashlight she'd grabbed from their bedroom.

Flashlight in hand, Dad climbed the rickety ladder and stuck his head up through the opening.

"There's nothing up here but some old boxes," he reported.

"Are you sure?" I asked.

"Come see for yourself," he said, climbing back down to the floor. He handed me the flashlight, and I nervously started to climb up to the attic above. Getting just high enough to poke my head through, I swung the light beam around to take a look. Dad was right. The attic, which ran the length of the house but was only about four feet high, contained a few old boxes but little else. There was certainly no sign of human habitation, let alone a trapped girl.

"Well?" Sara asked. "Any bodies up there?"

"Nothing," I said with a sigh. I wasn't sure if it was a sigh of relief or one of frustration. If the girl I'd heard wasn't in our attic, then where *was* she? And how long could she survive before someone came to help her?

....

I was deep asleep when I suddenly became aware of someone shaking my shoulder.

"Get up!" my dad shouted. "Hurry! We have to get out of here!"

Groggy from sleep, I propped myself up on my elbows and tried to focus my eyes. It was still pitch dark in the room. My bedside clock read 3:52 A.M. I sniffed the air. It smelled strange. Like smoke.

"What's going on?" I groaned.

"The house is on fire!" Dad said, grabbing my arm and pulling me out of bed. "I think the hot water heater short-circuited. We've got to get out! Fast! Get your shoes on and grab your jacket! Hurry!"

Mom was already helping Sara get on her robe as I

stumbled out of bed and searched for my shoes. Looking through the bedroom doorway, I could see a weird, flickering orange glow on the wall near my parents' room. It immediately made my heart switch into overdrive. I'd frequently had nightmares about being caught in a fire. Now it was happening for real!

"What about our clothes?" Sara asked.

"We can always buy new clothes," Mom assured her, "but I can't buy a new you. Let's get out of here!"

Barely a minute after Dad had rousted me from bed, all four of us were thundering down the stairs heading for the front door. Looking back, I could see that the entire end of the house was already in flames. Part of the kitchen was burning, and the air was thick with smoke.

Coughing and choking, we stumbled through the front door out into the cold, damp night. Dad fumbled for his car keys as we headed for our minivan.

"Shouldn't we call the fire department?" Sara asked.

"We already did," Mom replied, "but it's going to take them at least twenty minutes to get here from town. They told us to get a safe distance from the house in case the fire spreads to the woods."

Dad opened the sliding door for Sara and me. I was about to get in when I heard a girl's voice call through the darkness. "Help me!" she cried. "I'm in the house! I'm in the attic! Please, don't let me die!"

"She's still in the house!" I shouted to my parents.

"Who's in the house?" Dad asked.

"The girl!" I exclaimed. "The girl in the attic! We have to help her!"

"No!" said Mom. "There's no one up there!"

But it was too late. I was already running back to the house. I could just imagine some poor, confused girl trapped in our dark, cramped attic going out of her mind as the air became stifling hot and smoke curled up through the floorboards. I knew I couldn't let her die like that. I knew I had to help her.

When I got back to the cabin, the fire had already spread to parts of the main living room. I had to shield my face with my arms to protect myself from the intense heat as I made my way to the stairway. Choking on the smoke-filled air, I stumbled my way up to the second-story landing, opened the linen closet door, and found the pole with the hook on it.

"Lisa! Don't! Come back!" The voice was my father's. I looked back but could no longer see the first floor because of the thick smoke. If he was coming after me, he was going to have a hard time finding his way through all the soot and ash that filled the air.

Pole in hand, I reached up and, after two tries, found the pull ring. I yanked down and the springed latch released. The panel swung down and the ladder extended. I grabbed hold of a wooden rung and began to climb.

It was pitch dark in the attic. I hadn't brought a flashlight with me, so I couldn't even see as far as the end of my nose.

"Hello?" I called. "Is anybody up here? You have to get out! The house is on fire! I'm here to help you!"

On my knees, I began crawling along the floor, groping my way through the inky blackness. The floorboards felt unnaturally warm. Clearly, the fire was getting close. If I was going to save the girl, I'd have to save her fast.

"Don't be afraid!" I called into the void. "Let me help you! We have to get out of here!"

Just then, the entire house shifted slightly and I was thrown off balance. At that same moment the access panel in the floor swung shut and locked with a snap. Alarmed, I turned and retraced my steps, feeling about for the trap door. I began to cough and wheeze as the air began to grow thick with smoke from the fire below. Finally I found the panel, but I couldn't make it budge.

"Oh no!" I cried aloud as I realized that the lock could only be released from the other side. "Help!" I shouted. "Help me! I'm in the attic! Let me out!"

I pounded frantically on the panel, but I couldn't get it to move. The smoke was growing thicker, and I could barely breathe. "Help me!" I screamed again, louder. "Don't let me die in here!"

Just then, a cold shudder ran through my body. I'd heard those words before. They'd been shouted by the girl in the attic, the girl who'd drawn me up here in the first place. And then the horrifying truth hit me.

I was the girl in the attic! I hadn't been hearing voices from another place. They'd been from another time! I'd been hearing my own screams, the screams of my own death!

"No!" I cried, tears running down my cheeks. Balling my fists, I pounded furiously on the panel. I turned and kicked with all my might.

Crack! The panel began to split. I kicked again. With a sickening snap, the hinges broke free and the panel dropped out of sight.

And just as it did, a ball of searing flames exploded up

through the rectangular opening. The fire was already on the second floor. It was all around me and I was trapped. There was no way out.

The girl in the attic was indeed going to die.

Rules is Rules

C amp Elkhart was supposed to be a fun place for kids. At least that's what my mom and dad told me. The camp was up in northern Minnesota and had everything from baseball to go-carts. The place even had its own lake where kids could go swimming, fishing, and boating. What more could a kid ask for, right?

Well, my friend Kevin Blayne wanted more. He wanted better food. He wanted firmer mattresses. But most of all, he wanted *freedom*.

"Frank, this place is like a prison," he complained to me after our first week at camp. "They got rules for *everything*. They got rules for when you can eat. How *much* you can eat. What paths you can hike on. How far you can swim.

What time you have to go to bed. Heck, if I wanted all these rules, I'd have joined the army."

Of course, being only thirteen, Kevin wasn't exactly ready to enlist in the military. Still, even I had to agree that the guy had a point. The man who owned Camp Elkhart, a big, hairy ex-police lieutenant named Vince Mancuso, was *very* strict, and he passed this same no-nonsense attitude on to his counselors. Kids who disobeyed the rules were "denied privileges," which could mean anything from losing a night's dessert to being confined all day to the bunkhouse.

The rule we all hated was the one that said we had to bring all our boats in off the lake by five o'clock. This made no sense to us, since in northern Minnesota the sun didn't even set until around nine o'clock during July. Why waste four good hours of daylight?

One day we finally confronted our counselor, a tall, blond-haired college athlete named Mitch Logan, about this stupid rule.

"Hey, rules is rules," Mitch replied in his typically ungrammatical fashion. "We got 'em for a reason. For your own protection. You break the rules and awful things can happen to you."

"Like what, no pudding after dinner?" my friend Kevin asked sarcastically.

"Hey, don't be a smart aleck, Blayne," Mitch shot back. "A few years ago a bunch of kids broke the rules and, well, let's just say they won't be coming back to this camp ever again."

"What's that supposed to mean?" I asked. "You mean, they're dead?"

"I didn't say that," Mitch said defensively. "Just keep your nose clean, don't ask too many questions, and everything'll be just fine."

Kevin wasn't satisfied with Mitch's lame scare tactics and one day decided to see what could possibly happen to someone who had the guts to break one of Camp Elkhart's primary rules.

The next day, around 4:00 P.M., Kevin approached me while I was deep into trading baseball cards with some of our bunkmates.

"Hey, Frank, let's take a boat out on the lake," Kevin suggested. It had been a really hot day—the afternoon temperatures had climbed well into the 90s—and a trip out onto the cool, spring-fed lake sounded like a really good idea to me. But then I looked at my watch.

"We'd only have an hour," I said. "Remember, all the boats have to be off the lake by five."

"We'll have plenty of time," Kevin said with a mischievous grin. "Trust me."

Excusing myself from the knot of card traders, I followed Kevin from our bunkhouse down the winding trail to the rocky lakeshore. There we found three aluminum rowboats sitting on the water's edge, their paddles already in place.

"Come on. This'll be fun," Kevin said as he tossed me a bright orange life preserver. "I can't wait to get on the water."

Together, Kevin and I pushed the lightweight rowboat off the beach and onto the smooth, calm water. We quickly jumped aboard, barely getting our sneakers wet, then took positions on opposite ends of the small boat. Kevin, who had assumed the stern position behind me, grabbed the oar handles and began to row at a slow, steady pace.

"Ah, this is the life," I sighed as I leaned back, turning my face toward the blazing sun.

"Sure beats doing homework," Kevin agreed. "Hey, how 'bout we row to the other side of the lake and back?"

"Do we have time?" I asked, again glancing at my watch. We had rowed the mile-long trip many times, and it usually took us at least 45 minutes to make the full circuit.

"No problem," Kevin said with a devious look in his eye. He turned the boat directly away from the camp and continued to row at a slow, steady pace.

We reached the opposite shore twenty minutes later. Unlike most of the lakes here in northern Minnesota, this body of water had no development around it other than Camp Elkhart. There were no vacation homes. No corporate lodges. Not even a campground. There were only pine trees, oaks, and thick forest underbrush.

I'd always found this rather odd. When everyone was building vacation homes, why hadn't anyone developed this place? The lake itself was cool and clean, and the surrounding countryside was gorgeous. There was access to Interstate 30 just a few miles to the south, so it wasn't like the lake was in the boonies. Why, then, was Lieutenant Mancuso the only person to ever build here?

Again, I looked at my watch.

"It's a quarter to five!" I cried. "We gotta get back before we get in big trouble!"

"Don't sweat it," Kevin said, lying back with his hands laced behind his head. "It's time someone stood up to Lieutenant Mancuso and his stupid rules."

"Hey, you can do what you want, Kev, but why drag me

into it?" I protested. I plunked myself down on the seat next to Kevin and grabbed the oar handles.

"What do you think you're doing?" Kevin challenged.

"Taking us back," I announced as I dug the oars into the water.

"No way," said Kevin as he grabbed for my right hand.

"I don't want to get in trouble," I insisted as I continued to row us back toward the distant beach.

"I'll take the full blame," Kevin offered.

"Why would you do that?" I asked.

"Because I want to show them that people can be on the lake after five without anything bad happening," Kevin explained. "Wouldn't you like to be able to go boating after dinner? I mean, what's the point of having a lake if you can't use it when you want to?"

I considered my friend's argument for a moment. I had to agree that the five o'clock curfew did seem a bit much, if not downright ridiculous. Still, was it worth getting Lieutenant Mancuso and Mitch Logan mad at me just to make a point?

Before I could reply, Kevin yanked the starboard oar out of its mooring and tossed it into the water.

"Hey, what are you doing?" I cried in disbelief.

"Now it really *is* my fault," Kevin announced. "I lost the oar. We *couldn't* get back in time."

"You really *are* nuts, you know that?" I said.

"Exactly. And there's no point in arguing with a crazy man," Kevin said with an exaggerated smile. Once again he laced his fingers, slipped them behind his head, and lay back against the side of the boat.

My anger rising, I moved myself to the edge of the boat.

"What are you doing?" Kevin demanded.

"I'm going to get the oar," I said, checking the buckles on my life vest.

"No, you're not," said Kevin. He grabbed the end of my T-shirt and gripped it tightly.

"Let me go," I ordered.

"Not 'til you sit down and shut up," Kevin replied. "Can't you see I'm trying to make a point?"

I gave a frustrated sigh and gazed across the water at the cabins of distant Camp Elkhart. From here I could see the other kids moving about, some coming in off the baseball field, others heading for the mess hall for dinner. A few kids were waving at us, signaling us to come in off the water, but all I could do was just sit there and weakly wave back.

Frustrated, I again looked at my watch. It was now 5:10.

"Now we're really in big trouble," I sighed. I could just imagine Mitch sentencing me to kitchen cleanup duty for the remainder of my four-week stay. Kevin didn't seem to mind. He still leaned back, hands laced behind his head, looking like a kid who didn't have a care in the world.

Suddenly there was a deep *thump* and the boat rocked to one side.

"What was that?" I asked in alarm.

"I don't know," Kevin said, bolting upright. "It felt like we hit something."

I peered over the boat's starboard side, trying to catch a glimpse of whatever it was that hit our hull. I suspected we'd struck a floating log or submerged tree trunk, but I saw no sign of either.

Thump! The boat was jolted again, this time with even greater force.

"We didn't hit anything," I realized. "Something hit *us*."

"You mean, like a fish?" Kevin asked.

"If it's a fish, it's a really *big* fish," I stated, still searching for a glimpse of our unseen attacker. I tried to imagine what kind of lake creature could be large enough to strike this boat with the kind of impact we'd felt. Kevin and I had fished this lake all week, and all we'd ever caught were perch and sunfish, neither of which was more than six inches long. There were rumors in camp that a few bass also lived in the lake, but so far no one had actually caught one of these fish. And besides, bass weren't known for slamming themselves into fishing boats. So, what the heck *was* this thing?

I turned nervously to Kevin, hoping my friend could provide an answer. As I did, I watched in mounting horror as a huge snakelike tentacle rose out of the water directly behind my bunkmate. Sickly purple in color and covered with dozens of large suction cups, the glistening snakelike arm slowly reached down toward Kevin's head. I tried to speak, to shout a warning, but fear had clamped my throat as tight as a bear trap.

"What is it?" Kevin asked, seeing the terror in my eyes. He turned around and, seeing the huge tentacle reaching down for him, let out a horrific scream.

Wham! The aluminum rowboat shuddered as it was suddenly lifted several feet into the air, then tossed aside like a child's toy. It felt like someone had slapped me hard in the face as I hit the cool lake water, and for several seconds I couldn't tell which end was up. Fortunately my life jacket was strapped on, and a moment later my head bobbed to the surface, allowing me to grab a lungful of air.

Spinning around, splashing water madly, I watched in unspeakable terror as my friend Kevin thrashed wildly about, trying to free himself from the grip of the huge tentacle that had now wrapped itself around his body like a boa constrictor enveloping a hapless rabbit. "Help! Help!" he screamed, but his cries were cut short as all the air was brutally squeezed from his chest. Then something rose out of the water directly beneath the tentacle. I glimpsed it for only a second, but it looked like a mouth at least three feet in diameter and studded with several rows of sharp, triangular teeth. The tentacle lowered Kevin's twitching body directly into the monster's waiting mouth. A moment later it was all over. The mouth was gone. The tentacle was gone. Kevin was gone. I was all alone in the water. Even our rowboat was nowhere to be seen.

············

I couldn't say how I managed to get back to shore. I wasn't sure how long I'd remained floating motionless in the water, and I didn't remember swimming to the nearest shore or stumbling through the shadowy woods back to camp. One minute I was alone in the middle of the lake, the next I was staggering into Camp Elkhart's mess hall where the other kids, already finishing dinner, stared at me like I was a creature from another planet.

"Kevin . . ." I managed to force out of my constricted throat. "Kevin's dead."

The other kids just stared at me in dead silence. And no wonder. I knew my hair was a mess, my clothes were dripping wet, and my eyes were eerily dark and hollow. All the color I'd gotten from weeks in the sun must have completely drained from my face.

Mitch Logan rose from his chair and hurried over to me. "You were out on the lake, weren't you?" he whispered in my ear.

"Kevin . . ." I repeated, my voice shaking. "Something got Kevin . . ."

"Come with me," Mitch said, turning me away from the others. "We're going to see Lieutenant Mancuso."

I was still so scared that it took me nearly an hour to tell the whole horrific tale to the retired police detective. As Mitch looked on, I told the man everything. How Kevin had talked me into going onto the lake after four o'clock. How he'd thrown the oar overboard. How the huge lake monster had risen up and plucked my friend out of the boat like an appetizer off a silver party platter.

I was surprised by Lieutenant Mancuso's reaction. Or rather, his *lack* of a reaction. As I told my incredible tale, he just stared at me with his dark brown eyes, his expression unchanging. It was like this was the story he *expected* to hear, like I was giving just another routine police report. It took me a while to understand the reason for the man's indifference, and when I figured it out, it chilled me even more than the lake water had.

"You knew that monster was out there, didn't you?" I said, looking at Lieutenant Mancuso accusingly. "That's why no one else has built anything on this lake. It's 'cause of the monster. You knew about it, too, but you let us play on the water. Why? How could you do that?"

I was now so worked up that I was nearly hysterical.

"We told you, no sailing after five o'clock," Mitch

reminded me. "Nothing would have happened if you had followed the rules."

"You mean, that thing only feeds after five?" I asked in disbelief. "This has happened before, hasn't it? To those other campers you told us about. Well, thanks for sharing!"

"It was a boating accident," Lieutenant Mancuso said softly.

"What?" I asked.

"You and your friend Kevin were on the lake together," Lieutenant Mancuso said matter-of-factly. "Kevin dropped one of the oars. He reached over to get it. He fell in the water. He wasn't wearing his life preserver. He drowned. It was a terrible, terrible tragedy."

"But that's not what happened!" I protested.

"Sure it is," Mitch stated, his voice flat and robotlike. "Accidents happen. That doesn't mean that you shut down the whole camp, or that Lieutenant Mancuso has to lose his whole life savings. No, this camp has to keep going. For everybody's sake."

I didn't bother to reply. I could see from the cold, hard look in Lieutenant Mancuso's eyes that he was going to stick to his story, no matter what. He had all the money he ever saved tied up in this camp, and there was no way in the world he was going to give it up. If it cost the lives of some kids every few years, that was just too bad.

It was enough to make me want to throw up.

"It's getting late," Mitch said, pointing to the wall-mounted clock. "Almost ten o'clock. Curfew. Time to get in your cabin."

"Sure," I said softly as I rose from my chair.

"I'll call Kevin's parents tonight and tell them the bad

news," Lieutenant Mancuso said. "And I'll tell them you did everything you could to save your friend."

I merely nodded as I turned and headed for the door.

I was halfway to my bunkhouse when I felt the need to say one last, final farewell to my departed friend.

Overwhelmed by a deep sense of loss, I walked down to the lakeshore, walked out onto the deserted pier, and looked out over the wide, empty lake, its still waters reflecting the light of the bright full moon.

"I'm really gonna miss you, Kevin," I said, my eyes welling up with tears. "You shouldn't have died like that. We should have known about the monster. I mean, this camp shouldn't even *be* here. I don't care what Mitch says. I'm gonna tell people the truth. I owe you that much."

Filled with a new sense of determination, I turned away from the lake and headed up the dirt pathway back to my cabin. But when I got to the wood frame building, I found that the door was locked.

"Hey, open up," I said, knocking on the door. "It's me! Frank!"

"You know what time it is, Frank?" Mitch asked from the other side of the locked door. I glanced at my glowing watch face. It read 10:03.

"So I'm three minutes late," I protested. "What's the big deal? Let me in!"

Just then, I heard movement in the nearest bushes. Something was moving in the inky darkness. Something large. As large as a man. Or bigger.

"Come on, Mitch, let me in!" I demanded, my voice now choking with fear. I pounded my fist angrily on the door.

"Curfew is ten o'clock," Mitch stated. "We got reasons

for these things. You can't say you weren't warned."

Something snarled close to my ear. Sweat pouring down my face, I spun about to find myself staring into two hot yellow eyes. They were neither the eyes of a person nor of an animal. They were the eyes of something monstrous. Something evil.

"Sorry, kid," Mitch said just as the monster targeted its claws on my throat. "But rules is rules."

Sound Bites

Hunter Smith was singing to me. Just to me. All I could do was sit there, still as a statue, as Hunter's steel-blue eyes bore directly into mine, his long wheat-brown hair hanging heavily over his sweat-covered face, and his rough yet heavenly sweet voice piercing straight into my soul. Behind him, guitars screamed like tortured banshees and drums boomed like cannons, sweeping me up into a dizzying whirlwind of powerful emotions. I felt as if I were in a dream, a dream from which I never wanted to awaken. Such was the power of Hunter Smith's music.

"Jeanne!"

Someone was calling my name.

"Jeanne Ingersoll!"

I tightly closed my eyes, hoping that whoever this visitor was, he'd leave before Hunter's magical spell was broken.

"Jeanne, turn down that music!" My father was now shouting directly into my ear. Although Hunter Smith's voice still blasted through my bedroom, the man himself had disappeared, replaced by a mere two-dimensional color poster taped to my closet door. "Are you trying to blow up the house?" my father asked angrily.

Before I could reply, Dad stormed over to my shelf-mounted stereo and snapped off the power. My bedroom was instantly plunged into eerie silence. At that moment I felt as if someone had just torn my heart from my chest.

"What are you doing?" I cried. Leaping off my bed, I made a desperate lunge for the stereo, but my father, who was a good five inches taller than me, grabbed my outstretched arm and brought me to an immediate halt. "Let me go!" I demanded, struggling to pull free.

"No more music," my father said, his voice now little more than a whisper. I knew he was very, very angry. "It's almost nine o'clock. Enough is enough."

"This is my room," I insisted, finally yanking my arm away. "I can do whatever I want."

"This may be your room, young lady, but it's still my house," my dad countered. "And as long as you live under my roof, you'll live under *my* rules."

I couldn't help but roll my eyes. He'd used that "This is my house" line hundreds of times before and, frankly, it was getting a little old.

"Are you listening to me, young lady?" he asked.

"Yeah, I hear you," I said with a weary sigh. "Look, all my homework's done. I don't want to watch TV. I just want to listen to my music. What's wrong with that?"

"What's wrong is that you have the volume cranked as loud as a jet engine," Dad said, turning down my stereo's volume knob. "I can feel the whole house shaking, even downstairs."

"That's the way you're supposed to listen to rock music," I explained. "You don't just hear it. You have to *feel* it."

"Maybe you do, but *I* don't," Dad said. "It's so loud that even the neighbors are starting to complain."

"Fine," I said, knowing this was one argument I wasn't going to win. At least not tonight. "I'll use headphones. Will that make you happy?"

"No, I don't think so," said Dad.

"Why not?" I asked in surprise.

Without saying another word, Dad held out a piece of paper. I recognized it immediately. It was my first-quarter report card: one B, five C's, and a D.

"So?" I asked innocently.

"So this is the worst report card yet," Dad said, his face as hard as stone.

"Hey, I'm in eighth grade now," I said. "Things are a lot harder now. Plus it's my first quarter. I still need time to adjust."

"No, what you need is to buckle down, put your nose to the grindstone, and stop listening to that awful music," Dad said sternly. "I think it's rotting your brain."

Rotting my brain? For an instant I had an image of Grandma Rita, my dad's mom, in the nursing home shortly before she died. For years she'd had what I used to think was called "old timer's disease," but what I later learned was actually Alzheimer's disease. The disease had eaten away at her brain to the point where in the months before her death, she didn't recognize me, didn't recognize Dad, and didn't even know where she was. Seeing her cold, empty eyes staring off into space used to give me chills. Although she was still breathing, it was like she was already dead. Rock music hadn't done that to her, that's for sure. And it wasn't going to do it to me.

"I'll do better next quarter, I promise," I said sincerely.

"I know you will," my father replied. "Because between now and then, no more music."

"What!?" I practically screamed.

"Just what I said," Dad stated calmly. "All this time you spend listening to music is distracting you. You're thirteen years old now. You're not a child anymore. You have to start taking life seriously."

"You can't take away my music," I said through clenched teeth. I could literally feel the rage boiling up inside of me, ready to explode like an erupting volcano.

"It's for the best," Dad insisted.

"But my music is who I *am*," I insisted, tears now welling up in my eyes. "It's a part of me. It's in my bones."

"Well, your bones will have to do without for a while," Dad said dismissively. "At least until you're back to getting a B average. And that's the end of this discussion."

With that, Dad turned and left the room. I stood there in shock for several seconds, like someone who'd just taken a bullet in the chest and was waiting for her brain to start registering the pain. Finally the realization that my music was gone hit me in the face like a bag of wet sand, and I fell back onto my bed shaking from head to toe.

How could Dad do this to me? How could he take away

my *music*? It was the one thing I loved. The one thing I *truly* loved. The last time I'd felt this bad was when my mother died from cancer five years ago. Since then, it was hard enough for me to find something that made me happy. Music had done that for me. It had brought me comfort, hope, and inspiration. It had given me a reason to live. And now Dad had taken that away from me, just for the sake of some lousy junior high grades no one would even care about ten years from now.

I felt like I wanted to die.

• • • • • • • • • • •

"I just *love* Hunter Smith," Paula Lipton gushed.

"I know," Vera Pancheck agreed, her eyes focused somewhere a million miles away. "Sometimes I feel like he's singing just to *me*."

The three of us were gathered in the grassy courtyard just outside our school's cafeteria. It was lunch period and, with a good ten minutes left before the start of our next classes, we'd gotten together to listen to Hunter's new album on my friend Paula's CD player. It was a little awkward passing the headphones from girl to girl, but having been denied music for days now, I appreciated any little taste I could get.

"Hey, how 'bout we go to your house after school and listen to it together?" Paula suggested to me.

"Yeah, you've got the best stereo system in the city," Vera agreed.

"Can't," I said sadly. "My dad still won't let me listen to music. He says it's 'rotting my brain.'"

"What a jerk," said Paula. "I wouldn't let him get away with it."

"Isn't that, you know, *child abuse*?" Vera asked.

"It's your constitutional right," Paula said. "Freedom of expression or something."

"I'd sue him," Vera concurred.

It was good having friends like Vera and Paula. When things got bad—like when my mom died—I could always count on them to support me.

"I can't do that," I said, feeling somewhat helpless. And then an idea hit me. "But what I can do, Paula, is go to *your* house and listen. I'll just tell my dad I'm going with you to the library to study."

"Sounds great," Paula said happily. "You know, sometimes parents are so stupid."

"You said it," I agreed. Already my mind was racing to concoct even more ways to get around my father's ridiculous new rule.

....

I did spend that afternoon at Paula's house listening to the new Hunter Smith CD. It was his best album yet, and I couldn't wait to buy a copy of my own. I ran out that same evening and bought one at our local Music Mega Mart with some baby-sitting money, snuck my portable CD player into my backpack, and listened to the music on the bus, between classes, during study hall, and even during lunch. I don't think Dad had the slightest idea what I was doing. And even if he did, what could he have done to stop me? I was thirteen years old. He couldn't watch me every minute of every day. Vera was right. Parents *are* pretty stupid.

Two weeks after my father had established his pathetic "no music" law, I was lying in bed trying to get to sleep, but I couldn't relax. I'd spent every free minute of that day secretly listening to my Hunter Smith CDs, and his music was echoing through my head like a radio that refused to be turned off. I shut my eyes and tried to relax, but all I could hear was Hunter's tough, beautiful voice soaring above the whine of his backup guitars and the gut-pounding rhythms of his drums.

I imagined myself at one of his sold-out concerts, standing in the front row surrounded by hundreds of other wild, adoring fans. The spotlights were nearly blinding. I could feel the crowd pressing in around me and smell sweat hanging heavy in the air.

And there was Hunter Smith, standing not twenty feet away from me. Dressed head-to-toe in leather, he gripped his microphone like a man clinging to a life preserver in heavy seas, holding on for dear life as he poured his heart and soul into his song. And he was singing to me. Just to me. As I stood there totally enraptured, he slowly walked toward me, his right arm outstretched, his eyes blazing blue, as he shared with me the most passionate music ever heard on this planet.

I felt like I'd been lifted off the ground and transported to another plane. Never before had two souls connected this way. It was a kind of magic, the kind of magic that only music can create.

Ka-WANG!

I bolted upright in my bed, startled by a blast of sound I couldn't identify. Was it a thunderclap? An earthquake?

Had there been some kind of explosion, right in my house?

Ka-WANG!

There it was again. But this time I recognized the sound immediately as the ultra-amplified scream of a rock-and-roll guitar.

Almost immediately, my room shook with the low, bass-enhanced *thump-thump-thump* of a rock band's percussion section. Then the air exploded with the combined sounds of electronic keyboards, saxophones, and rhythm guitars. And above it all, soaring like an eagle on a mountain breeze, was the voice of Hunter Smith.

I immediately glanced over at my digital alarm clock and saw that the time was 2:12 A.M. I struggled to focus my eyes and get my bearings. *Who could be playing music at this hour?* I wondered.

The music felt like it was coming from right there in my bedroom. Thinking that my stereo had somehow turned on by itself, I climbed out of bed and stumbled over to my bookshelf. The stereo was dark and cold. I put my hand over one of the speakers and felt nothing. This wasn't the source of the music.

Next I went to my window and yanked it open. If the music had been coming from another house or a passing car, it would have gotten even louder when I did this. But the volume remained the same—thunderously oppressive.

"Who's playing that music?" I asked aloud. It wasn't that I didn't like it—heck, it was Hunter Smith!—but at two in the morning? Even to me, that seemed a bit much.

Now wide awake, I left my bedroom and headed downstairs to the first floor. I thought that perhaps my dad had learned that I'd violated his orders, that I'd been listening to music while away from home, and cranked up the stereo in the family room just to teach me a lesson. But when I got to the den, the stereo there was as cold as the one in my bedroom.

So where was the music coming from? It didn't make any sense. No matter where I moved around the house, the volume never changed. It was like the music was *following* me everywhere I went!

I hurried back upstairs in a panic and, without knocking, ran into my dad's bedroom.

"Huh? What is it?" Dad said, awakened by my entrance. "What's going on?"

"It's that music!" I shouted over the scream of the guitars and the pounding of the drums. "It woke me up!"

"What music?" Dad asked, his voice almost a whisper.

"What do you mean, *what music*?" I asked in disbelief. The volume now seemed even louder, and I had to put my hands over my ears just to hear myself think.

"Jeanne, if this is some kind of joke . . ." Dad began, obviously irritated.

"You mean you really can't hear it?" I asked in amazement. I was so scared that tears were pouring from my eyes.

"No," Dad said. "What do *you* hear?"

"It's Hunter Smith!" I shouted, barely able to hear myself. "From his new CD! It sounds like I'm standing next to a ten-thousand-watt speaker! I can feel it thudding inside my whole body!"

Just then, the awful realization hit me. The music *was* inside me! It was just like I'd told Dad last week. The music was a part of me. It was part of my soul. *It was in my bones!*

47

But unlike my stereo, my body didn't have an off button!

"Help me," I pleaded, dropping to my knees. The music was even louder now. My ears hurt. My head felt like it was going to explode. "Turn it off! Please, Daddy, make it go away!"

Dad was on his feet now. He was saying something, but I could only see his lips move. His voice was completely drowned out by the music blasting through my head. I squeezed my eyes shut, trying to shut it down by sheer force of will, but the music was far too powerful. It had taken over my body—or maybe I'd allowed it to take over. Whatever the cause, there was nothing more I could do but let it sweep over me, to take me to another plane, another dimension.

To a place of madness.

Night Terrors

No! Stay away from me! Help! Help! Help!"
Doug Snow bolted upright in his bed. His attention
turned immediately to his bedside clock. The glowing
numbers read 11:57 P.M.

Dazed and disoriented, Doug slid out from beneath his
covers. His heart pounding in his ears, he stumbled toward
his bedroom door. Although the screams that had jarred
him from his sleep now seemed like nothing more than the
echoes of a bad dream, he knew that they had come from
the adjacent bedroom. They were his father's. The man was
in danger. Perhaps he was fighting for his life.

Still too confused to fear for his own safety, Doug
stumbled into the main hallway of his family's one-story

ranch-style home and snapped on the light. He could hear faint movement from his parents' bedroom, which stood at the end of the corridor. The door was wide open.

"Dad?" Doug called softly. "Dad, are you all right?"

A figure immediately appeared in the bedroom doorway. It was his mother, a dark-haired woman of medium height who was dressed in pajamas and a familiar yellow terry-cloth robe. Adjusting her plastic-rimmed glasses, she gave Doug a warm smile.

"It's all right, Doug," she assured him, her voice soft and soothing. "Go back to bad."

"But I heard Dad scream," Doug insisted.

"He was having a nightmare, that's all," his mother explained. "He's fine now. It's late. You need your sleep."

"Okay," Doug said with a sigh. Turning back, he saw his younger sister, Lanie, leaning against her bedroom door frame.

"What's going on?" the nine-year-old asked.

"Dad had a bad dream," Doug said, assuming an air of authority. "Go back to bed."

With that, he snapped off the hallway light. Almost in unison, the three bedroom doors closed shut. Silence once again settled upon the Snow house.

It was exactly midnight.

· · · · · · · · · · ·

"How come you screamed last night?" Doug asked his father the next morning at breakfast.

Doug's dad, who was wearing a well-tailored blue pin-striped business suit and a colorful Italian-knit silk tie, nervously ran his hand over his nearly bald head and cleared his throat. "Actually, I thought your mother was a burglar," his father admitted.

"I stayed up late to watch one of the talk shows," his mother explained. "When I walked into the bedroom, it scared your father."

"Daddy's a scaredy-cat! Daddy's a scaredy-cat!" Lanie chanted tauntingly.

"Don't make fun of your father," her mother scolded. "You've had a few bad dreams yourself, as I recall."

Doug studied his father's face. The man seemed unusually tense this morning. There were dark bags under his eyes, and when he lifted his coffee cup, Doug could see his hands shaking ever so slightly. Doug began to suspect more was going on here than just a bad dream. But he decided it was best not the press the matter. Not yet, anyway.

···········

"No! Stop! Help! Ahhhhh!"

Doug's eyes snapped open. He was staring directly at his bedside digital clock. The time was 11:48.

Listening carefully, he heard faint voices coming from the room next door. His parents' bedroom. The voices sounded frightened. Upset.

Fully alert, Doug climbed out of bed, slipped on his leather house slippers, and padded over to his bedroom door. Peering down the corridor, he could see a faint light coming from the far side of his parents' bedroom door, which was only partially closed. Curious, he hurried to the door and whispered, "Dad? Mom? Are you all right?"

"We're fine, Doug," his mother replied. "Your father had another bad dream, that's all. Go back to bed. We'll see you in the morning."

"You're sure he's okay?" Doug inquired.

"I'm fine," his father assured him. "Now, please, just leave me alone."

Doug turned back to his room. It had been three days since his father's first nocturnal scream-fest. Every night since, his dad had woken up just before midnight screaming his head off. It didn't matter if his mom went to bed at the same time his dad did or not. Like clockwork, the nightmares came. And they were driving Doug crazy. These midnight cries weren't just mild grunts or moans. They were the loud, blood-curdling shrieks of a man who was truly screaming for his life. It didn't matter if they were just triggered by dreams. Doug's dad's nightmares were going to give *him* nightmares, and he wanted them to stop. *Right now.*

···········

"Are you having a hard time at work?" Doug asked his father the next morning as the older man prepared to leave for the office. Doug was referring to his father's job as a senior project manager for a major semiconductor manufacturing company.

"Not especially," his dad replied as he checked the contents of his leather briefcase. "We've been under a lot of pressure to finish our latest chip prototype, but we've still got plenty of time. Why?"

"Well, I once read that stress can cause nightmares, and I

thought maybe that's why you've been having these bad dreams," Doug explained.

"I appreciate your concern," his father said with a warm smile, "but these things go in cycles. I've had them before. Don't you remember?"

"No," Doug replied in surprise. "When was that?"

"When you were about three or four," his dad said. "Actually, I've had bad dreams ever since I was a kid. I even sleepwalked when I was a teenager. It's just how I'm built, I guess. Some people gets ulcers. Some people get migraine headaches. I scream in my sleep."

"Isn't there anything you can do about it?" Doug asked. "Can't the doctor give you pills or something?"

"I don't want to take any medications," his father insisted. "I'm sure this phase will pass just like the others did. I'm just sorry my nightmares disturb you and your sister."

"Me too," Doug said. "They're creepy."

"You ought to see them from *my* side," his father said wearily.

∙∙∙∙∙∙∙∙∙∙∙

The bedside clock read 11:53 P.M. Lying awake, his nerves on edge, Doug watched as the numbers changed to 11:54. Although he'd gone to bed over an hour ago, he couldn't sleep. He knew his father was going to scream again, and just knowing that any minute now the house would be filled with those horrific cries was enough to keep all his nerves on edge.

"No! Stop! Ahhh! Ahhh! Ahhh!" Right on cue, his

53

father's screams shattered the night's silence. But this time, they were joined by another set of cries, his mother's.

"Stop it!" he heard his mother shout. "Stop it! Don't touch me! No!"

Sensing that something was seriously amiss, Doug bolted out of bed and ran straight to his parents' bedroom. In the dim ambient light, he could see his mom and dad sitting up in bed, their heads bowed and breathing heavily.

"Are you okay?" Doug asked, concerned. "Mom, I heard you screaming."

His mother reached over and turned on her bedside lamp. At first the light hurt Doug's eyes, but as they adjusted, he could see a large red welt forming near his mom's right eye.

"What happened to you?" Doug gasped in shock.

"I'm so sorry," his father whispered, his voice shaking. "I thought you were someone else."

"Did Dad hit you?" Doug asked in disbelief. His sister, Lanie, was now at his side. She, too, was shocked by the sight of their wounded mother.

"He was having another nightmare," their mother explained. "He started swinging his arms. I tried to stop him, and that's when he hit me in the eye."

"I dreamed that people were chasing me," Doug's father stated. "I was trying to run away, but my legs wouldn't move. I had to fight back any way I could."

"I really think you should see a doctor about this," Doug said seriously. "Before you hurt Mom again."

"I agree," Doug's mother said.

His dad bowed his head sheepishly. "Maybe you're right," he admitted.

"Good," Lanie said. "Then maybe we can *all* get some sleep around here!"

············

The pills Doug's dad came home with the next day were prescription drugs designed to put the user into a deep, dreamless sleep. "The doctor says he's given these to other nightmare sufferers, and the success rate has been about eighty percent," he told the family over dinner.

"What about the other twenty percent?" Doug asked skeptically.

"I guess they still get nightmares," his dad said with a shrug. "But even if I still do have bad dreams, maybe I won't move as much."

"Or scream?" Lanie asked hopefully.

"Or scream," her dad replied with a smile.

"Well, I guess this means we'll all sleep a little easier tonight," their mother said.

"I hope so," Doug said. He was looking forward to a long, uneventful night.

············

"Arrrrr! Arrrr! Arrrr!" The screams coming from the room next door barely sounded human. They sounded more like the roars of an angry bear or a bellowing lion.

"No! Stop!" came another set of cries. Doug immediately recognized them as his mother's.

"I guess the pills didn't work," Doug said to himself. He imagined his dad once again flailing about in bed, striking out at enemies that existed only in his dreaming mind.

Crash! Something shattered in his parents' bedroom. It sounded like a lamp. Another sharp *crash* followed a few seconds later, accompanied by his mother's wild, terrified screams.

What the heck is going on in there? Doug thought. This sounded far worse than anything that had gone on before. Shaking from fear, Doug threw back his covers and hurried toward the source of the disturbance.

"Mom!" he shouted as he raced down the hall. "Mom, are you okay?" Along the way, he flicked on the hall light, bathing the entire area with bright luminescence.

Reaching his parents' room, he pushed the door open wide, allowing the light from the hallway to spill through. What he saw caused him to stop dead in his tracks.

His dad was out of bed, on his feet, and holding a golf club he'd grabbed out of the open walk-in closet. He was swinging the club wildly, his glassy eyes seemingly focused on something a million miles away.

"Wake up!" Doug's mother shouted as she ducked behind her side of the bed. "Bert, please, wake up!"

Crash! The framed picture hanging over their bed shattered as the golf club slammed into its protective glass. It took a moment, but Doug quickly realized that, although the man's eyes were open, his father was still asleep. Apparently, the sleeping pills he'd taken had worked *too* well, keeping him unconscious when he'd otherwise have been awakened by his own violent actions.

"Dad, wake up!" Doug shouted. "Put down the golf club!"

His father turned away from the bed and stared at his

son with cold, dead eyes. A moment later his face twisted into an evil sneer and, raising his golf club high, he charged in his son's direction.

"No!" Doug screamed. His arms held protectively over his head, he turned to run. He didn't see Lanie standing directly behind him. Brother and sister immediately collided, and both tumbled painfully to the floor.

"You won't get me!" their father shouted madly as he swung the golf club wildly through the air. Doug could feel the wind of the club's head passing as it *whooshed* no more than six inches from his head and slammed into the wall with an explosive *bang!*, creating a deep dent in the painted plasterboard. Lanie screamed as their father swung again, this time clipping the top of Doug's tangled hair.

"Leave the children alone!" Doug heard his mother shout. Looking up, Doug saw his mom grab the golf club from behind her husband and attempt to wrest it from his hands. His dad fought back like a maniac, still clearly in a dream state and totally unaware of what he was doing.

"Stay here," Doug whispered to Lanie. There wasn't much chance of his sister moving. At this point she was completely paralyzed by fear.

Hopping to his feet, Doug dashed into his bedroom. Looking about for a weapon, he grabbed the first heavy object he could lay his hands on—his piggy bank. Returning to the hallway, he found his mom and dad still locked in a struggle over possession of the potentially lethal golf club.

"Dad, this is gonna hurt me more than it'll hurt you," Doug said, sucking in a deep breath. "Or maybe not."

With that, he brought the ceramic bank down on the

back of his dad's head with a resounding *crash*! Quarters, dimes, and nickels went flying everywhere along with shards of painted fired clay. Stunned by the impact, his father stood rock-still for a moment. Then, like a felled pine tree, he swayed slightly and collapsed in a heap to the carpeted floor. Doug was surprised to see a slight smile frozen on his dad's unmoving lips.

....

"No more sleeping pills," Doug's dad announced as he poured the rest of the prescription drugs into the toilet. Doug, his mother, and his sister, Lanie, applauded as the man pushed the flush lever, sending the pills spinning into watery oblivion. He then rubbed the bruise on the back of his head, straightened his tie, and turned to his wife. "So," he said, "what's for breakfast?"

....

Doug's bedside clock read 11:56 P.M. Doug lay on his back breathing steadily, his muscles slowly relaxing. He was just beginning to drift off to sleep when he heard a terrifying scream emanating from the next room. "No! Ahhhh! Help me!" his father screamed. This was immediately followed by a sharp *slap!* as his mom woke the man from his nightly nightmare.

This ritual had become so familiar that Doug had learned to count on it, and now found it as comforting as a good-night kiss. Assured that he and his family were all safe and sound, Doug turned over in his bed, closed his eyes, and let himself fall into a calm, restful sleep.

Faces

Crash!

The explosive sound of shattering glass snapped Samantha Collier's concentration away from the homework on her desk and toward her bedroom window. There she saw her blue-and-white-striped curtains billowing ghostlike as a steady breeze whipped through the jagged hole in what had moments before been a pane of double-glazed glass. Countless transparent shards lay on the carpet beneath the window, glistening like diamonds, and in the center of the debris sat the cause of this mess: a scuffed Little League regulation baseball.

"Great," Samantha moaned as she rose from her chair. Brushing aside her long blond hair, she carefully picked up the ball, dusted off several tiny bits of glass, then looked out through what remained of her bedroom window. In the fenced-in yard next door stood two fifth-graders, Tommy Parker and Stewart Boggs. Tommy, the skinny one, was wearing a baseball glove. Stewart, who seemed to grow chubbier by the day, was holding a bat. Both were wearing expressions of extreme embarrassment.

"Ah, hi, there, Samantha!" Stewart shouted up at the window, waving to her.

"Can we have our ball back?" Tommy yelled.

Samantha's reply was cut short by a flash of light, followed by a crash of thunder. Tommy and Stewart immediately bolted for the house, and a moment later it began to rain.

············

"This should hold you until we can get the window replaced," Mr. Collier said as he tacked the plywood board into position. "I know it doesn't look very pretty, but at least it will keep the rain and bugs out."

"Thanks, Dad," said Samantha. She was sitting cross-legged on her four-poster bed staring at the ugly plywood rectangle that now blocked out her room's only source of natural light. She suddenly felt that her room had become a dungeon, that the board had sealed her off from the outside world. "How soon do you think I can get my window back?"

"The repairman said he's pretty backed up right now," her dad replied. "He said it will probably be about a week."

"I hope Tommy and Stewart are paying for this,"

Samantha said, her eyes now fixed on the wooden board. "It was their baseball, you know."

"Oh, they're paying for it, all right," her dad said with a knowing smile. "Their parents are making sure of *that*."

"Good," said Samantha. Her parents had raised her to own up to her mistakes, and she hated to see other kids get away with not taking responsibility for their actions. "Too bad they can't make the repairman come any faster."

"I know. It's a bummer," her father agreed. He looked at his daughter. "Dinner should be about ready. Coming down? Mom's barbecuing chicken."

"In a few minutes," Samantha replied. "I've still got some math homework to finish."

"Don't take too long," her dad said, heading for the door. "You know how much work your mother puts into her Thursday night barbecues."

Yes, Samantha knew all about her mom's barbecues. Although they could have easily afforded a propane grill, her mom always insisted on charcoal briquettes and mesquite wood chips. "Sure it takes longer," her mother always said, "but it sure makes the meat taste a whole lot better."

With the smell of the barbecue already wafting through the air, Samantha climbed off her bed and walked over to the plywood that covered her window. Something about it had disturbed her the moment her father had brought it into her room. It wasn't just its inherent ugliness. And it wasn't the fact that it blocked her view of the world beyond. No, there was something else about this board. Something creepy that she couldn't quite put her finger on.

And then she saw them. At first they looked like two

ordinary knotholes, the kind found in just about any wooden plank. But as she looked closer, she realized that they weren't just knotholes—they were *eyes*. Stepping back, she saw that these "eyes" were framed by a series of lines and swirls that combined to form a nearly perfect face. A catlike face. Above the eyes were a pair of angular whorls that became slanted eyebrows. Between the eyes was a ripple that doubled as a triangular nose. Below that was a twisted mouth and even a recognizable jawline.

The arrangement of these features was too perfect to be just her imagination. It was as clear and distinct as the four faces on Mt. Rushmore. Even more unsettling, the face seemed to be staring directly at Samantha. It seemed to *know* she was there, just as she could discern its presence within the wood.

"Dad!" Samantha shouted, her voice cracking with fear. "Dad, come here right now!"

She immediately regretted summoning her dad. She knew exactly what he was going to say. For this wasn't the first time Samantha Collier had seen a face where a face didn't belong. For as long as she could remember, she'd seen faces staring at her from the oddest of places. From the ceiling. From the wallpaper. From the clouds.

To most people, these "faces" that Samantha saw were nothing more than random patterns of shapes and shades found in everyday objects. They were just dots in acoustical ceiling squares, flecks of black in a linoleum tile floor, or the natural lines and swirls found in a wooden desktop.

But Samantha knew better. These faces were real. They represented life-forms that other people—through blindness or a simple refusal to believe—failed to see.

When Samantha was a child, she would often cry in terror when one of these faces suddenly appeared to her out of a bathroom floor or from within a billowing cloud. Now, in middle school, she usually kept these "sightings" to herself. But this one was different. It was so obvious and so disturbing that she couldn't stay silent.

"What is it, darling?" her father asked as he stepped back into her room. "What's wrong?"

"Look at this board," Samantha said, pointing at the image, her voice trembling. "Do you see it?"

"Do I see what?" her dad inquired, moving to his daughter's side.

"The face," Samantha said. "There's a face in the wood."

Her father examined the wood from one angle, then another. He shrugged his shoulders innocently.

"Sorry, honey," he said. "I just see a piece of wood. And you know why? Because that's all it is. A piece of wood. Your mind's playing tricks on you again."

She knew her dad would say this. Her dad *always* said this. Why couldn't he see something so obvious?

"But it's *there*!" Samantha insisted, pointing to the board. "See? There are the eyes. And the nose. And the mouth . . ."

"I've told you before, it's an optical illusion," her father explained. "The human brain likes familiar patterns. And one of the first things we come to recognize as babies are faces. So when we see something that even remotely has a symmetrical design, we tend to put a human face on it. Some people see faces in ink blots, or in parking meters. Some people have even seen a face on one of the mountains on Mars!"

Samantha closed her eyes and tried to push the horrible

image out of her mind. She took a few deep breaths, then slowly opened her eyes again.

The face was still there. It was looking at her. Studying her. Holding her in its sights.

"You're right," she lied, afraid her dad would think she was crazy. "It was just my imagination."

Samantha stayed close to her father as they both went downstairs to the kitchen. She said nothing more about the face all during dinner and remained silent on the topic when they later watched a movie on cable TV. But that night, when she went to bed, Samantha knew she was being watched. She tossed and turned in bed, trying to get comfortable, but she was constantly aware of another presence in her bedroom.

Finally she turned over and looked up at the plywood board that covered her window. At first, the board appeared to her as nothing more than a large black rectangle. But then, as her eyes adjusted to the darkness, details become clearer. Just as before, she could make out the distinct shapes of eyes, a nose, and a mouth. Even more disturbing, these features seemed to be *glowing* from within. It was as if they were trying to *burn* their way out of the wood and into the world beyond. Samantha's world.

Her heart beating wildly, Samantha turned away and buried her face in her pillow.

"It's just my imagination," she said to herself. "There's no face in the wood. My mind is playing tricks on me."

After a few minutes Samantha was finally able to relax. But even as she drifted off to sleep, she remained convinced that, here in her bedroom, she was not alone.

· · · · · · · · · · ·

Anne Besch was what many people might call "gothic." She preferred to dress mostly in black. Her hair, which was naturally medium brown, had been dyed the color of asphalt. When her mother allowed her to wear makeup, it was always very, very dark.

Like so many of the kids who were into the gothic movement, Anne was very much into ghosts, ancient spells, graveyards, and anything else that suggested the supernatural. Anne had long known about Samantha Collier's propensity for seeing faces where they shouldn't exist, which is why, even though they came from very different backgrounds, the two had long been best friends.

"Spooky," Anne said after Samantha told her about the glowing face in the plywood board. "That is, like, so totally cool!"

"I'm scared, Anne," Samantha confessed. It was lunch period, and they were sitting off by themselves in a far corner of the school cafeteria. "I know I'm just seeing things, but I can't shake the feeling that something is really there."

"Maybe it is," Anne said, raising a darkly shaded eyebrow. "You've heard of the Druids, haven't you?"

"I think so," Samantha replied. "Didn't they build Stonehenge or something?"

"Exactly," Anne said. "They were the ancient inhabitants of England. They worshipped nature. The earth. The sky. The seasons. They believed that the life force was everywhere, even in rocks. And they believed that spirits— intelligent spirits—lived in trees. That's why we still 'knock on wood' to ward off bad luck."

"So, what are you saying?" Samantha asked nervously.

"I'm saying that there really *could* be something in that board," Anne stated. "It could contain an ancient spirit, one that's fighting to get out."

"Do you think it's a good spirit or a bad spirit?" Samantha asked.

"Ah, now *that's* the final *Jeopardy* question, isn't it?" Anne said slyly. "What do *you* think? More importantly, what do you *feel*?"

Samantha didn't have to search her soul very deeply for an answer to that one. She knew *exactly* how she felt.

She felt afraid.

Very afraid.

....

"Who did this?" Samantha demanded. "Who did this to my room?"

She was standing in her bedroom doorway surveying a scene that could only be described as total chaos. It looked like a tornado had swept through her room, dumping all her books and papers on the floor, ripping apart her neatly made bed, and knocking the pictures on her wall askew. The plywood that normally covered the hole in her window was now lying crookedly against the wall, allowing a strong, cool breeze to blow in through the shattered glass.

"Oh, my," her mother gasped as she joined her daughter in the bedroom doorway. "This must have happened while I was at the hospital doing my volunteer work." She walked over to the plywood board, picked it up, and placed it back over the shattered window. "I guess the board must have come loose and the wind did this. You know we had that big wind blow through around noontime."

"No wind could have done this," Samantha insisted.

"Then what did?" her mother asked. "You think a burglar broke in, messed up your room, and then left without taking anything or touching anything else in the house?"

"No," Samantha said but left it at that. She was too scared to tell her mother what she really thought. Scared that her mother would think she was being a paranoid fool. Scared to admit the obvious even to herself.

She spent the rest of the day cleaning up the mess in her room, then collapsed exhausted in her bed around nine-thirty that night. Almost immediately the hairs on the back of her neck stood on end as she instinctively felt another presence in the room. Then she heard breathing. Heavy breathing. There was no longer any doubt: *Something* was in the room!

Alarmed, Samantha bolted up in bed and looked around. She appeared to be alone. Then she looked over at the plywood board. The face was back, even more distinct than ever. And its eyes seemed to be . . . *twitching*!

"It's just my imagination," Samantha said to herself in an almost ritual-like mantra. "It's just my imagination. It's just my imagination."

Slowly she rose off the bed, her right hand extended, and carefully approached the board. Foot by foot, inch by inch, she drew closer and closer to the strange, glowing face that seemed to be staring back at her from within the swirls of the wood's grain.

As her fingertips neared the strange, glowing image—
Snap!

The mouth literally jumped out of the wood and made a grab for her fingers. Samantha immediately yanked back her hand and gasped.

As Samantha backed away, continuing to watch in horror, the creature within the wood board slowly pulled its massive form out from the wood in which it had been imprisoned. First the head came free, its skull the size of a lion's but with a huge, forward-jutting jaw. Then its two front paws slammed down on the carpet, each foot armed with five thick, razorlike claws.

Oddly, although the beast's form appeared alive and supple, it still retained the look and texture of wood. Samantha could see the lines of grain in its skin along with the swirl of knotholes and the wavelike patterns of striations.

She knew there was no time to call the police. There was not even enough time to get her parents. If this beast was going to be stopped, she would have to do it herself—and do it *now*. But how?

The answer came to her in a flash. As the monster continued to squeeze its way into her room, Samantha turned and, slamming the bedroom door behind her, bolted down the stairs to the first floor. She flung open the patio doors and ran over to the backyard barbecue. She grabbed a can of lighter fluid in one hand, and a butane-powered charcoal lighter in the other.

Returning to her bedroom, she could hear something roaring and howling on the far side of the door. But there was no sound of movement. Perhaps the creature had not yet totally freed itself from its wooden prison.

Screwing up her courage, Samantha turned the knob,

then kicked open the door. Her heart nearly stopped when she saw, less than ten feet away, the form of a huge, catlike beast now almost fully formed.

Not allowing herself to consider the danger before her, Samantha entered her bedroom and immediately let loose a stream of lighter fluid in the beast's direction. The animal snarled and spat as its face became drenched with the strong, gasolinelike liquid, the substance soaking quickly into its pores.

The can *thunked* hollowly in Samantha's hand, and she realized it was now empty. She clicked the trigger on the butane-powered lighter. No flame. She clicked again. Nothing. Could it be out of fuel?

Gripping the instrument with both shaking hands, she gave one last, desperate pull.

Click! She was rewarded with a glorious, bright orange flame.

"Take *this!*" she shouted and hurled the wand at the wooden beast.

WHHHOOOOSH! There was an explosive blast of air as the monster's body burst into flames. Samantha ran back into the hall, slamming the door behind her. There was an explosive *bang!* as the creature hurled itself against the door. But the door held firm . . . this time.

"Samantha! What's going on?"

Samantha turned to see her mom and dad standing in their bedroom doorway looking dazed and confused.

"It's a fire!" Samantha cried. "We have to get out of the house! Now!"

At that same moment the beast howled and again threw itself against her closed bedroom door. To her parents, it must have sounded like a blast of wind bursting through her window to feed the raging inferno, but she knew the true source of the noise and knew there wasn't much time left.

"Move!" she cried and grabbed her parents by the hand. Too confused to resist, they followed their daughter down the stairs and outside into the damp night air. Just before leaving the house, Samantha turned and saw what appeared to be a giant cat, its body in flames, bounding down the stairs after them. She immediately leaped onto the porch and slammed the door, trapping the burning beast inside the home.

"Oh, no!" Samantha's mother cried. She was standing on the front walk looking back at their house. Flames were pouring from Samantha's bedroom window. More flames appeared behind the living room window on the home's first floor as fire from the burning monster spread quickly to the carpet, drapes, and furniture. "We're going to lose the house!"

"Better the house than our lives," Samantha said, more to herself than to anyone else as, *boom!*, the monster made one last effort to blast its way to freedom.

•••••••••••

Fairhaven Mental Hospital turned out to be far more pleasant than the stories that had floated around Samantha's hometown had led her to believe. The rooms were small but sunny. The doctors and nurses were all extremely pleasant. And the food, although not exactly delicious, was edible.

Samantha continued to wonder if it was smart telling the

police the truth about what had happened in her bedroom that awful night. She could have lied and said she'd just knocked over a candle, and that the fire was an accident. But she felt the world needed to know that, contrary to what parents always tell their children, there *are* monsters in the world. Of course, the police didn't believe her, so here she was spending day after day in her pajamas, attending countless therapy sessions as the doctors tried to cure her of an illness that she didn't even have. Yes, it was frustrating, but at least she was safe.

Allowing her mind to wander, Samantha settled back onto her pillow and stared up at the "popcorn"-style ceiling directly over her head. The room's low lighting caused the rough-textured material to create a complex pattern of tiny shadows. Although these shadows at first looked like nothing in particular, as Samantha continued to stare at them, something more familiar began to take shape. Something unsettling. Something frightening. Something that would give Samantha Collier nightmares for the rest of her days.

It was a face.

Scratcher

It was hot when Kent Newcomb awoke from a deep
sleep. *Real* hot. His pajamas were soaked with sweat,
and his pillow was uncomfortably moist from perspiration.

This was not a surprise. It had been blistering hot all
week. Afternoon temperatures had hovered around a
hundred degrees, and even at night the lows had failed to
get below seventy-five. The high humidity had made going
outside feel like stepping into a steam bath. As for sleeping,
well, lying on a bed of nails would probably have been more
comfortable.

Why is it that you always feel hotter at night? Kent
wondered as he kicked off his damp cotton sheet. His
blankets had long ago been banished to the floor. *I wish Dad*

would turn up the air conditioning. It's like an oven in here.

Kent turned his pillow over and tried to get comfortable. That's when he heard the noise.

Scratch. Scratch. Scratch.

It seemed to be coming from directly under his bed, yet at the same time seemed far, far away.

Scratch. Scratch. Scratch.

It sounded like a dog or cat was trying to claw its way through a door. But the Newcomb family didn't own any dogs or cats. In fact, the closest thing to a pet Kent had ever had was a box turtle he'd gotten for his seventh birthday, but it had long ago gone on up to that Great Terrarium in the Sky.

Scratch. Scratch. Scratch.

Kent sat upright nervously. A wave of dizziness swept over him, but it quickly passed. Knowing he could never sleep with that scratching going on, he got up, determined to find the source of the sound. At his bedroom door he paused and listened.

Scratch. Scratch. Scratch.

Whatever was out there, it was definitely an animal. But what kind? Maybe it was a squirrel that had somehow gotten itself trapped between the house's walls and was desperately trying to dig its way out. Or maybe it was a *rat* with pink, glowing eyes, a long, hairless tail, and fangs that were just itching to tear into human flesh!

Kent shivered involuntarily but resolved to press onward. He opened the door, ventured into the dark hallway, then paused at the top of the stairs.

Scratch. Scratch. Scratch.

The sound was definitely coming from downstairs. His

mouth suddenly as dry as sandpaper, Kent grabbed hold of the wooden banister and began making his way, step by step, down to the first floor.

Scratch. Scratch. Scratch.

The sound seemed to be coming from every direction at once. As he stopped to focus his mind, he realized that the scratching was coming from the far side of the breezeway door just off the kitchen. Beyond the breezeway was the home's laundry room and, beyond one more door, the two-car garage.

Now things were starting to make sense. Some kind of small animal must have found its way into the garage during the night, perhaps through an air vent or a crack in the wall that had otherwise gone unnoticed. It might have even scampered in when his dad drove his car in from work. Lost and unable to find its way out, the animal was now trying to free itself the best way it knew how—by digging through the house itself. But what kind of animal?

Scratch. Scratch. Scratch.

As Kent approached the breezeway door, he could feel rivulets of sweat run down his face. But it wasn't the heat that was making him sweat this time. No, the thirteen-year-old was *scared*. Some kind of wild creature was crouching in the darkness just a few feet away from where he was standing. Maybe it had rabies or some other dreaded disease. The last thing the boy wanted to do was open that door and let the creature come running into the house. But how could he make it go away?

Scratch. Scratch. Scratch.

His hand shaking, Kent reached for the light switch on the wall next to the breezeway door. He flicked it on and immediately saw a bar of bright light glowing through the crack between the door and the floor below. Instantly the scratching stopped and, for a brief moment, Kent thought he heard the sound of tiny feet clicking their way across the breezeway's linoleum tile. He stood there, barely breathing, for—well, he wasn't sure *how* long. Finally, after what seemed like an eternity but was probably closer to five minutes, Kent turned and slowly returned to the stairs. He made sure to keep the breezeway light on to keep the squirrel or rabbit or rat or whatever it was from returning.

Ten minutes later, Kent was back in his bed, slowly drifting back to sleep.

Scratch. Scratch. Scratch.

Kent's eyes snapped open like they were spring-loaded. He sighed with frustration. Something told him this was going to be a *long* night.

•••••••••••

"Yeah, it was some kind of animal, all right," said Kent's father as he and his son examined the inner face of the breezeway door the next morning. "Maybe there's a possum in the garage. Or even a raccoon."

Mr. Newcomb bent down to take a closer look at the door. The bottom right-hand corner was clearly marred by numerous scratch marks. In addition, the breezeway's tile floor was littered with wood shavings.

The inner door, the one that led to the garage, stood slightly ajar. They must have forgotten to close this inner door the night before, and that's how the animal had gotten into the breezeway.

"Do you think it's still in there?" Kent asked fearfully, turning toward the garage. He could just imagine some wild raccoon lurking in the shadows, ready to pounce on them at any moment.

"Hard to say," his dad replied. He opened the inner door all the way, reached through the doorway and flicked on the garage light.

Joining his father, the first thing that struck Kent was the stench. It smelled like rotten eggs, week-old fish, and really smelly cheese all mixed together in a big vat of sun-dried cat's guts.

Looking over to the garage's right-hand wall, he immediately saw the source of the awful smell. All three of the family's large plastic garbage cans were overflowing with trash. In addition, four large plastic bags, each bulging with more garbage, were piled near the garage door.

Kent remembered that their city's trash collectors had been on strike for the past two weeks, halting all garbage pickup in the area. As a result, refuse was piling up all over town, including in the Newcombs' garage. The aging trash and the recent record heat had combined to create an odor that was more repulsive than anything Kent could ever remember smelling. *No wonder we've started to attract wild animals*, he thought. *What self-respecting scavenger could resist a stench like this?*

The next thing Kent noticed was that the entire garage was strewn with stray bits of trash. Garbage was on the floor, on the cars, even in the storage shelves. It looked as if a wild monkey had rampaged through the garage throwing trash in all directions. Clearly, whatever their unwelcomed visitor was, it was capable of doing significant damage to the Newcombs' garage and everything inside it.

Kent's father pushed the button that activated the automatic garage door opener. Moments later the garage was flooded with bright morning light.

"Oh, no!" Kent's father cried as he stumbled over to his car, a late-model German-made luxury sedan. "Look what that thing *did*!"

Kent saw that his dad was pointing to several large scratches on the driver's side of the car.

"What do you think it was?" Kent asked.

"I can't think of any animal that can make scratch marks like that," his dad replied. "Except maybe a bobcat or a cougar. And those don't live around here."

"Do you think it's still here?" Kent wondered aloud, looking about nervously.

"It better not be," his father snarled, "or I'll kill it with my bare hands."

Kent looked about, searching for signs of movement. But all he saw was garbage, garbage everywhere. *It's probably gone*, he thought. *It must have gone out the same way it came in.*

Still, as his eyes surveyed the overflowing garbage cans and studied the shadows behind them, he couldn't help but get the uneasy feeling that he was being watched.

· · · · · · · · · · ·

Scratch. Scratch. Scratch.

Kent's eyes snapped open and he looked over at his digital alarm clock. It was just after two in the morning— and their nightly visitor had returned.

Feeling his heart pounding in his chest, Kent squeezed his eyes closed, pulled his pillow over his ears, and tried to block out the noise. But no matter how hard he tried, all he could hear was *scratch, scratch, scratch.*

We've got to get that thing out of the garage! he thought with alarm. *We have to get it before it gets us!*

Running on pure adrenaline, Kent threw back his sheet and stormed out into the hallway. Ten seconds later, he was back at the breezeway entrance. The night before, they'd made certain to close the breezeway's inner door, which meant the animal was now trapped in the garage itself. Kent pounded his fist on the outer door, hoping to scare it off.

"Go away!" he shouted. "Go back outside! There's nothing for you in here! Leave us alone!"

"Hey, what's going on down there?" he heard a voice demand. Startled, Kent spun around to see his father leaning over the stairway railing.

"That animal is back," Kent replied. "It woke me up. I was trying to scare it away."

"Well, you woke *me* up!" his father responded. "Your mother, too. We thought someone was breaking into the house!"

"Well, if you think about it, someone—or should I say, some-*thing* —is!" Kent noted.

Kent's father came the rest of the way down the stairs, then joined his son at the breezeway door.

"What are you going to do?" Kent asked nervously. "Open the door?"

"Shhhh," his dad replied, then put his ear to the door.

Kent held his breath as his father listened for sounds of movement in the garage. After about thirty seconds, his dad turned away from the door and toward Kent.

"Whatever it is, it's gone now," Kent's father said with a sigh. "Let's go back upstairs."

"But what about the animal?" Kent inquired. "I bet it's still in the garage."

"First thing tomorrow I'm buying a trap," said his dad. "Then hopefully we can all get a good night's sleep."

···········

The trap was about the size of a small microwave oven and was made entirely of wire mesh. Kent watched fascinated as his father demonstrated how the contraption worked.

"You put a piece of food, like this old piece of salami, here at one end of the trap," Kent's dad explained, laying the cold cut inside the device. "Then, when the animal walks in, it trips this little bar and—" *Clink!* The open end of the trap slammed shut.

"And it can't get out?" Kent asked.

"Not unless it can reach through the cage and flick this switch," his dad said as he pushed the little metal bar that opened the cage door. He then set the cage down in the garage in front of the breezeway entrance and set its door into the open position. "If our little friend shows up tonight, he's going to be very, very surprised."

"I hope so," said Kent as he gazed at the metal apparatus. Then a disturbing thought crossed his mind. "I just hope that cage is big enough. Would a cougar or bobcat fit in there?"

"I told you, wild cats don't live around here," his father insisted. "It has to be something small, like a possum or raccoon. Don't worry, this cage should be plenty big."

Kent's nose crinkled as he got another whiff of the stomach-turning stench coming from the trash cans. He wondered how even a wild animal could live in a place like this.

No wonder it's trying to get out, Kent thought. *If I was trapped in a place that smelled like this, I'd do anything to find my way out, too!*

• • • • • • • • • • •

"You open the door," Kent said as he and his father stood in the breezeway the following morning. His mother stood anxiously by the kitchen entrance about twenty feet away.

"If you *did* trap an animal, you'd better not let it in this house!" she said insistently.

"Don't worry, dear, it's not going anywhere," Kent's dad assured her. "I'll take it out to the woods and release it there."

"Well, let's see what we've got," Kent said eagerly. He watched his dad open the door to the garage, then snap on the light.

Kent couldn't believe the sight that greeted him.

The cage's door was locked shut, clearly indicating that something had tripped it during the previous night. But there was nothing in the cage but some old chicken bones and a few other stray pieces of garbage. Whatever had entered the cage had also found a way out, as impossible as that might appear.

"I don't believe it," Kent's father said as he examined the cage's door. "It's locked tight. There's no way an animal could have escaped."

"Maybe it's not an animal at all," Kent suggested. "Maybe it's a snake—something that could squeeze its way through the bars."

"Snakes don't leave scratch marks on doors," his father noted. "No, whatever it was, it must have run out of the cage *before* the door fell shut."

"Then how did all that garbage get in the cage?" asked Kent, pointing to the bits of paper, food, and other unidentifiable items that covered the cage's floor.

"I don't know," his dad replied. "I honestly don't know."

Together, father and son turned their eyes toward the shadowy garage beyond. Although Kent had no proof, he knew in his heart that their visitor was still with them—and was probably laughing its nasty little head off.

....

Years earlier, when Kent was in third grade, he thought it would be fun to spend the night sleeping in the family minivan. "Camping out," he called it. He set up a sleeping area in the back of the van, brought in a bag full of snacks, and listened to his boom box/CD player for entertainment. At nine-thirty, his parents turned off the garage light and told him to go to sleep. He was back in the house and in his bed fifteen minutes later.

Kent couldn't help but think about that incident as he now sat in the van's front seat surrounded by total darkness. This time he wasn't "camping out" but was "staking out" the garage so he could catch the creature in the act. Knowing he could never sleep through another night of that incessant scratching, he'd convinced his folks to let him spend the night in the minivan and wait for the elusive intruder to show itself. He figured that once they knew what kind of animal had invaded their garage, they'd have a better idea of how to deal with it.

Initially Kent found it difficult to relax in the van. Although he was inside the vehicle, the stench from the nearby garbage was still pungent enough to give him a headache. It was also very hot in the garage, and the lack of circulation made the atmosphere inside the van virtually stifling. But in time his nose got used to the smell, and he grew accustomed to the temperature inside the minivan. Pushing the front passenger's seat back as far as it would go, Kent was able to make himself comfortable enough so that, around midnight, he finally dropped off to sleep.

···········

Kent wasn't certain how long he'd been out, but all of a sudden he snapped back to wakefulness.

Scratch. Scratch. Scratch.

The sound was coming from directly ahead of him. Something in the garage was trying to scratch its way through the closed door into the breezeway.

Disoriented by the near-total darkness, Kent reached over to the steering wheel and fumbled around until he found the headlight controls.

"I got you now," he said softly, then flicked the knob at the end of the control stick.

Instantly the garage was flooded with blinding white light. A moment later he heard an ear-piercing screech and something landed on the hood with a *splat!*

At first Kent thought it was a large cat that was covered head-to-tail in garbage. The animal's entire surface was layered with meat scraps, chicken bones, soiled cardboard, orange peels, and other assorted trash that the Newcombs had thrown out over the last two weeks.

But when the animal leaned toward the windshield and glared at him through eyes made of slime-covered cellophane, Kent realized to his amazement that this animal wasn't covered with garbage—it *was* garbage! Somehow, the mounting pile of rotting refuse combined with the unrelenting heat had caused the various organic compounds in the Newcombs' trash cans to recombine and form the living horror that now stood just inches from his face!

Snarling through lips made of rotting meat, the creature used its razorlike claws—which seemed to be made out of bits of old aluminum cans—to tear at the windshield.

Terrified, Kent leaned as hard as he could on the horn.

Hoooonnnnkkk!

Startled, the garbage creature leaped off the hood, disappearing from sight.

Kent hit the horn again. Then again. Then a third time.

"Help!" he screamed, although he doubted if his voice could carry from inside the minivan. "Dad! Help me!"

He hit the horn again, praying that his father would respond in time.

A moment later the light came on in the breezeway and the door opened to the garage. There stood his father, wearing his pajamas and wielding a baseball bat.

"It's in the garage!" Kent screamed. "It's some kind of garbage monster!"

But as his father covered his eyes to shield them from the glaring headlights, Kent realized that his message was definitely *not* getting through the minivan's windows.

Realizing he had to talk to his father directly, Kent tried to lower his window. But since the minivan's motor was not running, the power window failed to respond as he pressed the switch back and forth.

"Look out!" he shouted.

Just then, something flashed through the air and landed on his father's chest. He heard his father scream, then fall to the floor.

With no consideration for his own safety, Kent grabbed the door handle and jumped out of the minivan. Running around to the front of the vehicle, he saw the horrible garbage monster standing on his father's chest, snapping and snarling like a wildcat. Holding the baseball bat with two hands, his father was just managing to keep the creature from plunging its teeth—which were made of everything from rusty nails to old fishbones—into his throat.

Searching for a weapon, Kent grabbed a garden shovel that hung from a hook on the wall.

"Get off my father, you piece of trash!" Kent shouted, then swung the shovel with all his might. When the blade connected with the creature's torso, Kent heard a wet, squishy *thwack*, much like the sound of a two-by-four slamming into a rotting pumpkin. The creature let out an ear-piercing shriek.

Garbage flew in all directions, and when the debris finally settled, Kent and his dad found themselves covered from head to toe with gobs of chicken fat, vegetable shavings, and bits of trash they couldn't even identify.

"What *was* that thing?" Kent's dad said with disgust as he slowly climbed back to his feet.

"I think I know, but you'd never believe it," Kent replied. Then he smelled his sleeve and nearly gagged. "I think we both need to take a shower."

· · · · · · · · · · ·

At his father's insistence, the Newcombs called the local animal control office and reported their run-in with what Kent was now calling the Trash Monster. The officer who took the report, a humorless woman in her late thirties, listened to Kent describe the incident and concluded that their attacker had been a stray dog that had simply gotten itself covered with refuse. As for Kent's theory that the creature had spontaneously come to life in their trash cans, she dismissed such an idea as "garbage."

Kent's parents had to agree with the animal control officer. After all, monsters don't just spring to life in people's trash containers.

However, Kent couldn't help but notice that, the next day, his dad ran out and bought an automatic trash compactor that sealed their garbage tight. And as he took the first of the hermetically sealed bags out to the garage, Kent also couldn't help but notice when—for just a brief second—the package seemed to move.

Shop Till You Drop

I gotta have it," said Casey Wrightwood.

The tall fourteen-year-old middle-schooler was pointing to a red silk blouse hanging on a rack of sports clothes marked 30% OFF! Her azure blue eyes blazed like twin suns, and she hungrily licked her lips as if she were gazing at the world's greatest ice cream sundae.

Her friend, Joleen Kloepfer, looked at the tag hanging from the blouse's right sleeve.

"It's a medium," she reported. "You take a small."

"I don't care," said Casey, grabbing the blouse off the rack. "Look at that color. The fabric is so soft. And best of all, it's thirty percent off! I'm telling you, I gotta have it!"

Before her friend could protest, Casey turned and raced

over to the checkout counter. The cashier, who didn't look to be much older than Casey herself, read the blouse's tag with a hand-held laser scanner, then announced the results. "That'll be $13.80, including tax."

Casey dug into her blue vinyl purse and produced three $5 bills.

"You're nuts, you know that?" said Joleen as she joined Casey at the counter. "When you get home, you'll put that blouse in your closet and you'll never touch it again."

"I know," Casey confessed sadly as she watched the clerk fold her new blouse and place it into a shopping bag. "But buying clothes is just so much *fun!*"

She collected her change, grabbed the plastic bag printed with the store's brightly colored logo, then headed out into the concourse of the Stratford Center shopping mall. The enclosed mall, with its brick-lined footpaths and groupings of thick ficus trees, was crowded for a Thursday afternoon. Many of the shoppers looked to be teenage girls much like Casey. *No doubt picking up something new for the weekend,* she thought.

"You know what your problem is?" Joleen asked. "You're a shopaholic."

"That's not true," Casey replied defensively, stopping in front of another junior fashion store to admire the window display.

"Yes, it is," her friend insisted. "You buy things you don't want, don't need, and usually can't even afford just to do it. It's like shopping makes you high."

"A shopaholic is someone who shops *compulsively,*" Casey corrected her. "They can't help themselves. I can stop shopping whenever I want. It's just that, well, I don't want to. In fact, I would shop forever if I could."

Joleen glanced at her watch. "It's almost five o'clock," she announced. "I want to get home soon. I've got math homework that's due tomorrow."

"All right," Casey said with a sigh. Scanning the surrounding storefronts, her eyes came to rest on the window of a small shop bearing the name Wishers. Its window was filled with numerous fashion accessories, including purses, scarves, bracelets, and various pieces of costume jewelry. A white-on-red banner hung over the window declared GRAND OPENING SALE—EVERYTHING 25% OFF! "But first, let's check out that new place," Casey said.

Before Joleen could protest, Casey was making a beeline for the new store.

"Five minutes," Joleen insisted. "No more."

Wishers turned out to be everything Casey had hoped for. Although only about 300 square feet, the tiny fashion store was crammed wall to wall with all kinds of kinky, colorful doodads, whatnots, and thingamajigs. With an expert eye, she quickly scanned the various rows of costume earrings, plastic bracelets, Day-Glo headbands, and neon-colored shoelaces.

"This place is *great*!" Casey gasped in awe.

"It's all junk," Joleen said dismissively.

"I know," Casey agreed. "But it's *great* junk!"

Looking about, she noticed a large bin standing in the corner. Piled within were dozens of small purses made of bright, shiny vinyl. The sign taped to the side of the bin read TODAY ONLY—ALL PURSES 35% OFF!

"Oh, my, my, my," said Casey, practically drooling. "Will you look at *this*!" She sifted through the multitude of purses that had been thrown haphazardly into the bin, then came up with one that was a dazzling ruby red. There was no other one like it in the pile. "I have *got* to have this purse."

"You already *have* a purse," Joleen reminded her. "In fact, you already have *ten* purses."

"Yeah, but I don't have *this* purse," Casey emphasized. She checked the price tag. "It was originally $21.95. Thirty-five percent off that would be $14.27."

When it came to mentally computing sales prices, Casey Wrightwood was a virtual Albert Einstein.

"How much money do you have left?" asked Joleen.

Casey checked her purse. "Only seven bucks," she replied, her voice tinged with disappointment. "Can you loan me a ten?"

"Hey, don't look at me," Joleen said, backing off. "I've been broke for the last week, remember? I only came here to watch *you* shop."

"Darn," said Casey, pouting. "I really liked this purse."

She opened the clasp to look inside. Immediately her heart skipped a beat.

"Look at this!" she whispered. She reached inside and pulled out a fresh, crisp $10 bill.

"It must be some kind of mistake," Joleen said.

"This is the kind of mistake I can live with," said Casey and immediately headed straight for the checkout counter.

"What are you going to do?" Joleen asked urgently, tugging at her friend's sleeve.

"I'm going to buy the purse," Casey stated. "I mean, it's 'finders keepers,' right?"

The way Casey figured it, there was no way to ever determine who the $10 really belonged to, so why not just recycle it back into the store? It wasn't like she was stealing or anything.

"Well, how do I look?" Casey asked after paying for the purse. She was now standing in front of Joleen with the red vinyl purse slung over her right shoulder.

"Like a girl who wants to go home," said Joleen hopefully, looking very, very tired.

"All right," said Casey, still bubbling over with energy. "I can't wait to tell the kids at school what a deal I got on this. Heck, it was practically a *steal!*"

Giggling at her own joke, Casey grabbed her shopping bags—one of which contained her old purse—and led Joleen back out into the mall.

They hadn't gone more than five steps when Casey suddenly stopped short in front of the Street Smart fashion boutique.

"Whoa! Look at that skirt!" she gasped, gazing at a lemon-yellow knit skirt on a mannequin display. "I gotta have it!"

"It's very pretty, but we don't have any more time, and you don't have any more money," Joleen reminded her. But it was too late. Casey was already heading through the shop's front door.

She ran directly over to a table where several knit skirts in various solid colors—yellow, red, blue, and orange—were neatly stacked. Without even looking at the size or price tag, she grabbed one of the yellow skirts and took it straight to the cashier.

She was waiting anxiously for the cashier to ring up her order when Joleen joined her.

"What are you doing, Casey?" Joleen asked sternly.

"You know you don't have enough for that skirt!"

"Will that be all?" the young cashier asked.

"Um, this, too," Casey replied. She impulsively grabbed a pair of socks off a nearby display and set them on the counter.

"You're crazy," Joleen said, nearly shrieking.

"That'll be $35.71," the cashier reported. "Will that be cash or credit card?"

Looking suddenly lost, Casey reached into her new vinyl purse, which of course she knew contained only the $2.45 she had left. But when she withdrew her hand, she was stunned to see she was holding two crisp new $20 bills.

"Um, cash," she said with a smile and handed the money over to the cashier.

"What's going on here?" Joleen asked, totally confused. "Where did that money come from?"

"I don't know!" Casey confessed. "It wasn't there before. It's like it just appeared by magic!"

"Let me see that," Joleen demanded. Before Casey could reply, Joleen grabbed the red vinyl purse, opened its brass clasp, and looked inside. All she could see were two $1 bills and some change.

"This is too weird," Joleen said, letting the purse go.

"I know," said Casey, now grabbing hold of three shopping bags. "But why look a gift horse in the mouth? I got a free skirt out of it."

"You didn't even try it on," Joleen reminded her as they headed out the door. "You don't even know if it fits."

"Who cares?" Casey said with a laugh. "It was free!"

A weird, almost maniacal smile broke out on Casey's face. Her skin had turned deep red, and beads of sweat were glistening on her forehead. Panting heavily, the girl looked like a runner who'd just completed a mile-long footrace. Joleen was getting nervous.

"Casey, I think there's something wrong with you," she said in a controlled, even voice. "I really think we should go home. Right now."

She reached for Casey's arm, but Casey pulled herself away, nearly dropping her packages in the process.

"No!" she shouted. "I have to keep shopping! I have to get as much as I can while this purse still works!"

"What?" Joleen asked in confusion. But it was too late. Casey was already stumbling toward the nearest store, which happened to sell home electronics.

Outside of her stereo and portable CD player, Casey had never had much of an interest in things electronic. But now she was practically burning with the urge to *buy, buy, buy*, and it didn't matter what it was.

Within ten minutes she'd bought herself a new telephone with a digital answering system, a miniature color TV, a calculator, a diver's watch guaranteed to work to a depth of one hundred meters, and a nonactivated cellular telephone. The cost—over $1,000—she paid with the cash that continued to pour miraculously from her red vinyl purse.

Next was a trip to a gourmet chocolate store where she plunked down over $500 for Belgian-made truffles, bon-bons, nut clusters, and chocolate-covered orange peels.

At the computer software store, she paid over $700 in cash for war games, flight simulators, and arcade-style shoot-'em-ups for a home computer she didn't even own.

She next bought a leather jacket that was three sizes too big for her, a pair of Italian-made shoes that were two sizes too small, and finally a diamond ring she couldn't possibly wear without everyone thinking she'd stolen it.

By this point Casey was almost impossible to see behind all the packages and shopping bags she was attempting to carry. She was stumbling through the mall like an overburdened camel who'd been out in the desert a week too long. Her legs hurt. Her arms ached. Her feet felt like they were on fire. But Casey didn't care. She just had to keep *moving*.

Pale and gasping for breath, she inched her way toward the nearby escalator while Joleen walked behind her, her arms folded sternly.

"Casey, you're scaring me," Joleen said.

"Gotta keep going," Casey gasped hoarsely. "Can't stop. Gotta keep shopping. Can't stop now . . ."

Joleen ran ahead and attempted to block her friend's path. "Casey, keep this up and you're going to kill yourself!" she said. "We've got to get out of here. It's like this mall has cast some kind of a spell on you!"

"Gotta keep shopping!" Casey snarled, shoving Joleen aside. Several packages went tumbling in the process, but Casey didn't react. It was as if she didn't care what she *had*. It was the act of shopping itself that was feeding her need.

"Give me the purse," Joleen demanded.

"No," Casey replied curtly.

"It's the purse that's causing this," said Joleen. "Give it to me and maybe you can save your sanity."

"No!" Casey shrieked, tightening her elbow's grip on the purse's leather strap.

Joleen made a grab for the red purse, but Casey turned away. Joleen grabbed for it again and this time got her hands on its slick vinyl surface. She tried to pull it free, but Casey's grip was iron-tight. It was as if Casey and her purse had become a single entity.

"No! No! No!" Casey screamed like a mother who was in danger of losing her baby.

Joleen noticed that other shoppers were staring at them and backed off. She watched sadly as Casey, her arms totally filled with packages, stumbled onto the ascending escalator. As Casey stepped aboard, she lost her balance and went crashing into the mountain of boxes and shopping bags in front of her.

"Casey!" Joleen shouted, then bounded onto the moving escalator after her friend.

Reaching the spot where Casey had fallen, Joleen had to literally dig through a pile of paper and cardboard until she could find her friend. She found Casey's arm buried under a department store shopping bag and grabbed her hand.

"Stand up," Joleen said.

"I can't," Casey said, her voice straining. "I'm stuck!"

Indeed, as Joleen dug deeper, she saw that part of the purse strap had wound itself around Casey's throat. But as Joleen bent down to remove it, the escalator begin approaching the top of its ascent. The moving stairs contracted into one another, and one of the sharp, toothlike ridges snagged the other end of the strap.

"Help!" Casey screamed in terror as she felt the vinyl strap quickly tighten around her throat. Choking for air, she grabbed the strap and pulled frantically, but it was no use. At the same time Joleen urgently searched her pockets for something to cut the strap with. All she could come up with was her set of house keys.

"Helllpppp!" Casey croaked as she was pulled closer and closer toward the escalator's metal teeth.

Without even thinking about what she was going to do next, Joleen grabbed what looked like the longest and sharpest of her keys and dug it into the hinge that connected the strap to Casey's purse.

"Hang on, Casey!" she shouted, her eyes nearly blinded by tears, as she tried to cut the strap loose.

Casey's eyes were bulging out of her head and her tongue was starting to turn purple when—*snap!* The strap suddenly tore loose, freeing itself from Casey's throat. Joleen immediately grabbed her friend by the hand and pulled her off the escalator to the landing above. A small crowd of shoppers had already gathered, apparently drawn by the irresistibly grisly sight of a fourteen-year-old girl being strangled to death by her own purse.

Looking back, Casey and Joleen watched as the red vinyl purse crumpled and was sucked into the escalator's upper mechanism. Seconds later the rest of Casey's packages came spilling onto the landing like luggage coming off an airline baggage chute.

"I think I wanna go home," Casey said softly as she slowly got to her feet. The wild look had suddenly vanished from her eyes, and the fever had gone from her cheeks.

"Good idea," Joleen said, steering Casey toward the exit.

"Hey, what about all your stuff?" one of the onlookers asked, pointing to the pile of shopping bags and boxes that had accumulated at the top of the escalator.

"That stuff?" Casey replied with a look of confusion. "It's not mine. I've never seen it before in my life."

....

It was nearly closing time at the Stratford Center shopping mall. Traffic at the Wishers store had dwindled to just a handful of people. One of them was fifteen-year-old high-schooler Lynda Bell. Picking through a bin of purses marked 35% OFF! she found, at the very bottom of the pile, a purse made of shiny red vinyl. It was the only purse like it in the entire store.

"Hmmm, looks nice," Lynda said, admiring the purse's liquidy sheen. Intrigued, she clicked open its brass fastener and looked inside. Immediately her face broke out in a broad grin and her eyes lit up hungrily.

For there, staring up at her invitingly, was a fresh, crisp new $20 bill.